Looking at Life

A Collection of Devotions, Poems, and Short Stories

ENDORSEMENTS

This book is very easy to read and a real page turner. Every short story and poem touched my heart in some way and left me wanting more. It's encouraging to know that God is working in so many lives and making good for those who love Him.

—**Richard W. Haines**, Author of *Spiritual Wingman: A Fighter Pilot's Journey to God*

Get with a great group of writers, and you're sure to find a lot of great writing. We encourage one another to excel, and readers reap the rewards.

—**Frank Ball**, Author of *The Discussion Bible and Eyewitness: The Life of Christ Told in One Story*

From beginning to end, this lovely book is a delight. Each individual story is engaging and unique, many speaking to me as a woman, a mother, a wife, and a daughter. The beautiful and thoughtful poetry interspersed throughout is the cherry on top!

—**Brandye Kiker**, Owner, Bookends, LLC

Looking at Life

A Collection of Devotions, Poems, and Short Stories

WOLF CREEK CHRISTIAN WRITERS NETWORK

PUBLISHED BY: Wolf Creek Christian Writers Network Press, 122 Peninsula Place, Pagosa Springs, CO 81147, 2019

Library Cataloging Data

Names: Wolf Creek Christian Writers Network (Wolf Creek Christian Writers Network)

Looking at Life: A Collection of Devotions, Poems, and Short Stories / Wolf Creek Christian Writers Network

178 p. 23cm × 15cm (9in × 6 in.)

Description: an eclectic collection of stories written by a diverse group of Christian writers from all over the country who now live in southern Colorado. Experience their adventures and share in their trials and triumphs in this moving, encouraging, humorous and inspiring work.

Identifiers: ISBN-13: 978-0-578-54158-7 (POD) | (e-book)

Key Words: Overcoming Adversity Christian Struggle, Colorado Senior Life Adventures, Inspiring Christian Short Stories, Real Life Stories Memories, Christians Starting Over, Memoirs High School Yesterday, Christian Memoirs Baby Boomers

DEDICATION

This collection of written works is presented for the sole purpose of giving all glory to God who inspired each of us through the Holy Spirit. May our words bless every reader.

———————⊶⊷———————

In memory of Beth Jayne, our beloved sister in Christ and fellow writer, who encouraged us with the following words:

"Keep writing! Keep getting the truth out there in all those amazing formats that we represent. Keep using your talent to draw people closer to Jesus. He's given you wonderful imaginations and creativity and possibilities. I am your cheerleader!"

ACKNOWLEDGMENT

Our sincere thanks to Betty Slade, Linda Farmer Harris and Richard Gammill for founding Wolf Creek Christian Writers Network (WCCWN). Our members are blessed by the education, encouragement and support we receive from each other every week.

We so appreciate our editors Terri House and former editor Carl Isberg of the *Pagosa SUN* newspaper who give us an opportunity to publish our works through Matter of Faith and Artist's Lane. This platform is an honor and privilege we will never take for granted.

Crossroad Christian Fellowship has provided a warm and welcoming home for our group for five years. We feel so blessed and thankful when we drive up on Monday mornings anticipating our time together.

Our talented book designer, Derinda Babcock, has been indispensable as she led us through the daunting process of publication.

And where would we be without Linda Farmer Harris, Kanaka Perea, and Elizabeth White? They shared their marketing savvy, web page and social media experience, and brought our group online.

And lastly the editorial team would like to thank the writers of WCCWN for the privilege of reading your work and curating the material for this book.

WCCWN Book Team

TABLE OF CONTENTS

Endorsements iii

Dedication vi

Acknowledgment viii

Foreward xii

Words, Joy Wiersma 1

The Lindas, Linda Farmer Harris 3

A Mutt, a Boxing Ring, and a Fight for Forgiveness,
    Peggy Bodde 7

Identity Crisis, Joyce Holdread 11

Love Never Gives Up, Richard Gammill 13

The Missing Book, Silver Mist 17

Glow In the Dark, Allyn Schuyler 23

Baron and the New Beginning, Peggy Bodde 25

October, Neal Johnson 29

Coasting or Competing? Gregg Heid 33

Star Song, Blythe McHatton 35

Don't Do It, Jesse Wenzel 39

Redemption, Peggy Bodde 43

A Fragile Heart, April Adamson Holthaus 45

Silence, Neal Johnson 49

DT, Gregg Heid 51

Saturday, Lynne Moffett 55

Cliff & Clara, Allyn Schuyler 61

Like a Lamb, Joyce Holdread 65

Like a Lamb Poem, Joyce Holdread 69

Be Brave, April Adamson Holthaus 71

Love, Diane (Graff) Cooney 75

Mandy's Solution, Linda Farmer Harris 77

What Was In Grandma's Purse? Betty J. Slade 81

Tests of Faith, Sylvia McDaniel 83

Can't Stop, Lynn Moffett 89

GOD'S NIGHTTIME RAINBOW, Diane (Graff) Cooney 91
THE SIGNIFICANCE IN MY SUNRISE, Paige Dené Wiersma 95
SNOWY TWIGHLIGHT, Joy Wiersma 97
THE BLESSINGS OF WISDOM, April Adamson Holthaus 99
OUR GRAND LADY: COLORADO, Betty J. Slade 101
BURIAL OF FREDERICK GEORGE SEBBACH, Pamela Sibback Hayes .103
NUTS FOR CHRISTMAS, Richard Gammill 105
4-F, Kathy Zilhaver 109
I WISH I HAD A GOAT LIKE THAT! Hank Slikker 111
SAVING ABBEY'S MOM, Kanaka Perea 113
A VERY PECULIAR ALTAR, Theresa Lussi 117
THE BLACKBERRY, Elizabeth White 119
A LETTER TO LISA, Beth Jayne 121
LOST AND FOUND, Jackie Henderson 123
LEPRECHAUNS, Dan Englund 129
THE PROWLING LION, Neal Johnson 133
MOMMY, DO ANGELS SMOKE? Hank Slikker 137
A CLIMB TO THE TOP, Theresa Lussi 139
GLISTENING NEW YEAR'S EVE, Beth Jayne 143
HIS WORDS, OUR WORDS, Jessica Tanner 145
AUTHOR BIOS 149

FOREWORD

Believing God has gifted each of us to write, the Wolf Creek Christian Writer's Network (WCCWN) has bonded together for encouragement and to hone our skills as writers. We are a Christ-centered community whose members include writers and editors across diverse genres and representing numerous denominations. Many of our writers have published books, screenplays, articles and blogs. Though we each may have different goals as writers, we are unified in our desire to stimulate people's thinking toward the relevancy and power of God's existence and love.

Betty Slade, Lin Harris, and Rich Gammill founded the WCCWN in 2015. Since then, the group has expanded and continues to grow with an average weekly attendance of 20+ writers.

Our weekly meetings always begin with prayer and a "From the Heart" presentation led by one of our writers. Every other week, we learn from one another via small critique groups and on the weeks in between, we benefit from advanced instruction in the craft of writing. Our instructors range from writers and editors within our group to outside speakers with experience in marketing, publishing and specific genres.

We welcome newcomers and invite you to visit our Facebook page (https://www.facebook.com/wolfcreekchristianwritersnetwork/) and website (http://www.wolfcreekwriters.com/) to learn more about our community.

WORDS

By Joy Wiersma

Beginning to the end
Words tell a story
Where everything is filled up
With a literate kind of glory

The warmth of affirmation
The cold of rejection
The joy of a happy ending
And the sorrow of lost direction

Words are a gift
That we couldn't live without
We're always thirsting for more
Like an unquenchable drought

The embodiment of soul;
A tiny bit of magic that we've caught
Our emotions written down
As a tangible thought

Spoken out loud
A noteless song
Something we take for granted
An art form almost completely gone

But words tell us a story
In the language of our heart
It isn't something we can control
But a journey on which we can embark

THE LINDAS

By Linda Farmer Harris

It wasn't just because I was facing emergency cancer surgery or that my cardiologist had found heart arteries seventy percent blocked. It was because I needed a word from the Lord especially for me.

I grew up in a Christian home, accepted Jesus Christ as my Savior at age eight, was a compliant, obedient child, and didn't experience the typical adolescent friction with parents and siblings.

I married a preacher and we had the daughter of our dreams. For 55 years, I watched the Lord do incredible things in my life and in those around me. His presence, promises, and provision were never in question.

That morning's devotional reading was about the heroines of our faith who risked life and limb in their walk with the Lord. The more I read the more I realized my own faith life paled in comparison. My witnessing testimony was plain vanilla. There had been no addictions to overcome; no, his, mine, and our children to cope with; and no estranged family to reconcile. I had no captivating stories to share that would rend hearts and draw people to Christ. Come to think on it, compared to my life, vanilla was a vivid, pulsating color.

I always wanted to be on mission with God, but things never seem to work that way for me. I'm a doer not a leader. I'm a top notch, over the top second banana. Yes, I've had my share of moments in the limelight and periodic accolades for services rendered, but I had nothing I could point to that filled my need to know that I was special to God or especially used by God. I felt like I was sailing along in the shadows of fellow Christians. At one point, I seriously questioned my salvation when everyone around me was having these life satisfying God-experiences and I was wondering if He even knew I was here.

Then I felt guilty because I selfishly wanted to experience God in a way that no one else could say, "My aunt Tilly had that same experience" or "That happened to me, too."

That morning, I sat in the pre-surgery cubicle with my husband, daughter, and pastor. Although my heart doctor was concerned enough to be standing by in the operating room during the uterine cancer surgery, I wasn't afraid of dying.

The first person to come in was a cheerful young woman in her mid-twenties. "Hi, Mrs. Harris, my name's Linda and I'll stay with you until they move you to your room after surgery."

"Your name will be easy to remember."

"My mother is named Linda, too."

I laughed, "Now, that's a hoot. Most Lindas don't name their daughters Linda."

After the lab technician drew blood and inserted the I.V. unit, Linda took my free hand and said to my family, "You can leave now, I'll hold her hand until you see her again." Jerry and Amanda gave me kisses and love ya's then left.

Everything happened very quickly after that. Linda was holding my hand when I went to sleep, and she was holding my hand when I woke up in recovery. Logic tells me she wasn't holding my hand during the actual surgery, but it was comforting to have her there when I woke up. It was like God was saying that He was holding my hand.

When I woke again, I was in my room. Linda was talking to another nurse and she still had my hand. When she was sure I was fully awake she said her goodbyes and the new young lady stepped over to take my vitals and introduce herself.

My laugh was more like a burp than the belly laugh I felt.

"Lynda" was the night nurse.

I drifted back to sleep chuckling to myself. Lynda was followed by Lynn and Lynn was followed by a new Linda, who was replaced by Lynne, who was replaced by a young oriental man, Lin, who turned me over to the check-out clerk named Lyndia.

I was overwhelmed. Everyone who touched me from check-in to check-out was named Linda or a derivative of it. The wheelchair attendant came for me and I expected to see the last "Linda" in the now familiar pattern.

I know my face reflected a bit of disappointment as Sue positioned the wheelchair for me to sit down. I told Sue about my "Linda" experience and how it had blessed me, how it felt like God had demonstrated his presence during my surgery and recovery.

For a moment, I thought I had offended her by speaking about God.

She leaned down and flipped over her "Sue" name tag over to show her full name. Linda Sue had chosen to use her middle name at the hospital – it was faster to write on charts.

Jerry and I talked about the Lindas in my hospital stay and how incredibly God had answered my prayer. Wow, now try and top that.

Two days later I went for my post-surgery check-up and was ushered into the examination room by a new nurse. I gasped when she lowered her clipboard.

Linda was a bit taken back when I laughed. From start to finish God called my name. He had made it abundantly clear that He knew my name and even though I felt insignificant, He felt differently.

I told the nurse my Linda story and we had a good laugh until she said, "I can top that."

I must admit that statement sent my heart into a tailspin. I know my smile looked pasted on because my heart didn't want to listen to her explanation.

"I don't work in this office. In fact, this is my first time here in the South Austin office. You're my only patient. When you leave I go back to the North Austin office. Looks like I'm here just for you."

I didn't know whether to laugh or cry.

There, just for me. What an awesome God we serve.

That evening's family Bible reading in Psalm 40 put everything into final perspective, especially verses 17.

"But may all who search for you be filled with joy and gladness. May those who love your salvation repeatedly shout, but I am poor and needy; Yet the LORD THINKS UPON ME. You are my help and my deliverer; Do not delay, O my God." (NKJV)

Not only is God thinking about me, even when I don't feel like He is, He calls me by name. What a mighty God we serve.

A Mutt, a Boxing Ring, and a Fight for Forgiveness

By Peggy Bodde

"You made all the delicate, inner parts of my body and knit me together in my mother's womb.... You watched me as I was being formed in utter seclusion, as I was woven together in the dark of the womb. You saw me before I was born. Every day of my life was recorded in your book. Every moment was laid out before a single day had passed." (Psalm 139: 13-16 NIV)

When I first laid eyes on these verses, I was dumbfounded. I read them again and again. Children who are abused or abandoned feel unwanted and deeply rejected, born into a circumstance of burden. I felt God's truth rolling over my wounds, a healing that comes with a certain amount of pain. These words spoke of purpose and a God who wanted me from the very beginning. God had intentionally created me, and his eyes were on me before I was ever born. But if his eyes were on me from the beginning, there was a childhood that had to be reckoned with.

I went to elementary school in Markham, Illinois. White people were in the minority, and though there were many different nationalities there, I was never sure where I fit in. I remember being in third grade and watching a small group of students on the playground standing around and calling each other names. They were older than I was and used ugly, racist words that I didn't like. One of them caught me staring.

"What are you staring at? You don't even know what you are. You're nothing but a mixed breed." He spat the words out and leaned in toward me, "A mutt!"

I narrowed my eyes, stiffened my scrawny arms, and stomped away angrily. He was right. I had no idea what I was. My skin was yellowish-brown. My eyes were almost black, but they weren't slanted up or down. My hair was dark-brown and stringy. I was adopted at birth by a Japanese woman and a white man into a household governed by fear and control and wallpapered in mental illness. There was never any room for questions.

My Adoption Story

Mrs. Wulf was full-blooded Japanese, and she resented me because I hadn't come from her body. She came from a wealthy family who had lost everything in the War. Promised to a cousin in an arranged marriage, she escaped that fate by coming to the states with Mr. Wulf, who was fresh out of the Army. He couldn't produce children, but because neither of them could speak the other's language, they didn't discover this problem until later.

After years of being childless, which was shameful in her culture, Mrs. Wulf agreed to adopt. They brought Linda home when she was less than a year old, a half-Korean and half-American baby. Three years later, I came into the household as a newborn: half-Chinese and half-Italian. Our adoptive parents knew our nationalities from the beginning, but they kept this information from us. Growing up unwanted in an adoptive home and knowing I wasn't fully American—but knowing little else—left me feeling a bit lost. A mutt. A loose end.

As I grew older, I began to realize that what happened inside our house wasn't normal. I started rebelling and threatening to tell, which led to my being booted out at age thirteen. To some this may seem scary, but to me—it was freedom. Freedom from the physical and verbal blows, freedom from trying to earn love, and freedom from a war I wasn't equipped for and didn't understand. The darkness in their home pressed me until I was thin and empty, and every step away from them was weighted with relief.

No government system or oversight was involved. Various families took me in along the way, and I rode that wave of grace through high school and college. Statistically, my life could look very different. I could have ended up homeless, a drug addict, or dead. Yet, when I was the most vulnerable, there was no shortage of safe havens for me. The time I spent in an unstable home environment had a beginning and an end, but finding forgiveness in the aftermath of suffering is never an open and shut case.

Into the Ring

Long after that season passed, I found myself face-to-face with the knowledge that perhaps I would never fully know why I suffered so much as a child. God is ultimately sovereign over everything that happens to us, which means he allows suffering, but he also redeems every experience. At some point in our faith journey, we find ourselves at a crossroads. A heart-stopping experience or epiphany forces us to deliberately choose to follow Christ or go the other way. In my case, this path toward Christ has meant spending numerous rounds in the ring, fighting my way through the realization that God is good even though I was adopted into an abusive home.

In between rounds, an imaginary person walks across the ring holding up a placard. Instead of a number, the placard always displays the same word, forgive—not a word that's easily packaged and tied up with a shiny bow. Round one: my adoptive family. Round two: myself for poor choices I made and blamed on my childhood. Round three: the God who didn't answer in the way I wanted during that deeply painful season of my life.

The Mess of Forgiveness

For most of my adult years, I was terrified to forgive. I thought forgiveness would require reconciliation. I thought forgiving would release my adoptive parents from accountability, and in my mind—that would mean I deserved what had happened to me. I cried the first time I asked God to help me forgive, because I didn't really want to. I wanted to hang on to the anger because it felt safe. I wanted to keep using my childhood as an excuse for the unhealthy relationships I seemed drawn to. If we sit in our wounds long enough, they become who we are.

I've since come to realize that God can handle my anger, and he is faithful and patient. He didn't abandon me or stop loving me when I admitted that some of my anger was directed at him. When I got serious about fighting for forgiveness and surrendering my past, he got into the ring with me. But unlike a sanctioned fight inside a boxing ring, mine goes on for endless rounds, and I may win some—but others leave me flat on my face. Forgiveness is messy and blurry and seems to run just far enough ahead of our faith to be out of reach. But in faith, we keep grasping. We keep surrendering, and we keep believing.

Father,

Thank you for going first: for your love and forgiveness that call us to follow suit. May our hearts reflect you. May the world see you. May our stories glorify you.

IDENTITY CRISIS

By Joyce Holdread

WHAT IF....

Apricots sprouted no fuzz,
And bulldogs had no frown?
If camels had no humps at all,
And ducks flew upside-down?

If the majority didn't always rule,
And nomads invaded Cuba?
If the octopus had *one* pair of pods,
And the piccolo grunted like the tuba?

If quack were the sound from a donkey's throat,
And Rabbis preached only on Sunday?
If gypsies settled in the Bronx,
And the weekend began on Monday?

If unicorns trampled the garden,
And the Vatican sanctioned the pill?
If wallflowers learned how to flirt,
And prunes, not pickles, were dill?

And if zebras weren't in the zoo,
But flew like striped Pegasus, high?
Would you, indeed, be you?
And I, uniquely, I?

Love Never Gives Up

By Richard Gammill

Kevin Adams put his arms around Alicia and pulled her close. "Our love has survived many crises. We will find a way to get through this one."

"Where did we go wrong?" said Alicia. "How did we fail our son? He was such a good child, and now this. How do we help him? These last three years have been horrible."

Twenty years ago, their love had welcomed little Eric into their lives. The childless couple peered at him through the maternity ward window and knew he was the one to fulfill their longing for a child. They took him home to a beautifully decorated nursery, completed the adoption process, and dreamed of their future together.

Eric fulfilled their dreams through his elementary school years; Kevin and Alicia agreed they could hardly imagine a more perfect child. Family life centered around their Christian faith, and Eric kept busy with school and church youth activities. In high school Eric had friends who introduced him to alcohol and cigarettes. He experimented but assured his parents he had taken up no bad habits.

A savings account had grown over the years, enabling Eric to enroll in college. His grades during his freshman year weren't outstanding, but his parents were hopeful. Two months into his sophomore year, a phone call from Eric shocked his parents. "Mom, I'm dropping out and coming home. I've been suspended and have to leave immediately."

"But what is it, Eric? What did you do to get in trouble?" Alicia could not imagine her son being expelled from college.

"Let me wait until I get home to talk to you about this."

Eric took two days to pack up and make the drive home. His parents prepared themselves to handle this situation with love and patience. Whatever Eric had gotten himself into, they would stand by their son.

When Eric's car pulled into the driveway, Alicia ran out the front door with outstretched arms. After their embrace, she looked at him. *He is such a clean-cut, good-looking boy. I couldn't love him more.* "Tell us what's going on."

"I've been using drugs for a long time now. I don't know how I kept up my studies last year. I had to sell some drugs to pay for what I needed, and that's what got me busted."

Kevin approached; his displeasure obvious. "Now what'll you do?"

"I guess I'll look for a job."

"What about your drug habit? Will you quit? Can we get you some help?"

"That's hard, really hard. I'll try. I don't want help, but I'll try to quit."

Eric piled his things into his bedroom. The hard rock music started immediately.

"Eric, this isn't going to work!"

"It's my room, and I need this music to calm my nerves."

A week later, Alicia answered the phone. It was Eric. "I'm at the police station I need you to come and bail me out. They're charging me with a DUI."

"Don't tell your dad about this. I'll get money from our savings and bail you out."

Every prospective employer required a drug test, and Eric failed repeatedly. He retreated into his bedroom and the house vibrated with his music.

Kevin's patience was quickly exhausted. "There's no peace in our house. We're not doing Eric any favors by tolerating this."

"Please, dear. Eric needs us to understand what he's dealing with."

"What he's dealing with is destroying our lives."

The phone call a week later was from a police officer. "We've just pulled your son out of a wreck. He's on his way to the hospital."

Eric's car was totaled, but he survived. The court sentenced him to thirty days in jail. Thirty days with no rock music in the Adams' house. Thirty days of endless discussions between Kevin and Alicia: how should they handle this?

"Eric can't live in this house if he won't change his behavior," Kevin said, his voice rising.

"But he needs us so much now. How can you kick him out?"

"Watch me."

Kevin relented, giving Eric another month to go straight. But there was another DUI while Eric was driving the family car. His sentence this time was six months in jail. When Eric was released, Kevin refused to let him come home. Alicia helped him find a room to rent.

"Alicia, what's happened to the money that was in our savings account?"

"Please don't be mad. I used it to bail Eric out of jail and pay his rent."

"Look at you! Eric is playing on your sympathy and destroying your health."

"But I love him so much, and I pray for him every day. I can't let him down. He needs me."

"We've lost the son we used to have, and now I'm losing my wife. This can't go on. I'm calling Pastor Jones. He'll talk some sense into you."

By the time their counseling appointment arrived, Eric was back in jail.

"Pastor, Alicia and Eric need to know I've had it. I'm done," Kevin said. "If Eric is determined to destroy his life, he's got to do it on his own. I don't want us to have anything more to do with him. I need you to tell Alicia to back off. I want my wife to be protected against what Eric is doing to her and to us."

Pastor Jones listened to Kevin and paused for a moment before responding. "You want me to support your decision to abandon Eric to his demons."

"If that's the way you want to put it—yes."

"That's a pretty extreme step."

"Maybe so. But we have been under extreme stress for three years now. We can't live this way. I can't stand what's happening to Alicia."

Alicia spoke up. "I want you to be more concerned about Eric than about me. Do you think I can just turn off my love and abandon him? He's lost—and who is there who really cares about him besides us? His druggy friends and drinking buddies are no help. Remember, you haven't always been perfect to live with, but I would never think of leaving you."

"That's why I love you so much—too much to let you keep being hurt by Eric."

"I need you to love me enough to let me love our son. I can't give up on him."

Both of them looked at their pastor. "That's how true love works," he said. "It never, ever gives up. It goes after the missing lamb, ignoring the risk and not counting the cost."

"I don't know, Pastor," Kevin said. "It seems way too hard and too painful. I'm angry with Eric and hurt by him. I wish we had walked away from that maternity window and left him there."

"Kevin!" Alicia blurted. "You can't mean that."

"I've thought it many times lately. But you're right. In my heart I don't mean it. I just can't handle this."

"There's no easy answer," Pastor Jones said. "Loving isn't easy, not in these tough situations. Not when it inflicts so much pain. The shepherd went after the lost lamb because that's what a shepherd's love requires him to do. It's never easy, but it's all the lamb has going for it. Otherwise, the lamb is doomed. The shepherd's love is the lamb's only hope."

Kevin looked down for several moments before speaking. "Okay, but God will have to help me. Humanly speaking, I'm done. But you say I can't give up on Eric. You preach that Jesus is the Good Shepherd. If Jesus loves Eric the way he is, then maybe he can help me do the same. We can't keep enabling his bad behavior, but we can love him."

Matthew 18:10-14, Luke 15:1-7: Parable of the Lost Sheep

THE MISSING BOOK

By Silver Mist

Author's Note: "The Missing Book" is a prequel story to a book series taking place in the realm, or world, of Alorren. The series, called *The Prophecy of Seven*, is currently a work-in-progress.

A firm shake of her shoulders woke Acna from her nap. She squinted in the afternoon sunlight to identify her intrusion. "Muriel?"

Muriel released Acna and nodded. The older woman's dark purple hair slipped from its up-do. "Acna, the book is missing. Lotta remembers Elloise dusting around the hiding place a couple days ago, but no one's been able to find Elloise."

Acna got up from her spot against a fruit tree's trunk and wiped dirt and old leaves from the bottom of her dark brown uniform. She straightened her off-white apron. "No one has seen Elloise for a couple of days?" The grogginess from her nap evaporated and her heart rate steadily increased. Two Caretakers of the Treaty of Alorren had mysteriously died in the last month. Many of the Caretakers were on edge, they feared the deaths could be a sign an ancient evil had awakened and was after their secrets.

Muriel, Acna's fellow servant of the royal family and her mother's friend, clasped and unclasped her violet-colored hands. "No, it's just for the past three hours we haven't been able to find her. Lotta went to ask Elloise about the old volume, see if she remembered where she put it or if she was the one to pick it up but…" She shrugged her shoulders.

Acna patted Muriel's upper arm. "I'll go find Elloise. Can you let Gretta know I'll be late getting back to my station in the laundry?"

"Of course." Muriel moved toward the main garden path. "Thank you, Acna."

Acna scanned the garden. Elloise was becoming more and more distracted. Part of that could be blamed on the woman's age, she'd recently turned 342, which was pretty old for a Grigorian. But Acna doubted age to be Elloise's trouble because when the older servant was asked about her activities, she would regularly tell of her latest adventure with her friends on the palace grounds.

A cool breeze flitted through the garden and played with the chestnut strands of Acna's hair. She needed to fix her braid before returning to work. But for now, she'd leave it alone. She explored the obvious hiding places, the paths, the fountains—even the groupings of plants. Where was Elloise? And where was the Grigorian part of the three-book peace treaty of Alorren and its various people?

A familiar figure in a dark green cape snuck through the garden.

Acna whistled a simple tune the red and yellow birds of the forest used. The person, Prince Zephner, stopped and turned toward her. He waved. She gestured for him to come over.

The cobalt skinned, sixteen-year-old prince slipped through bushes and past trees to her side. "Hello, Acna." He grinned. "Think you can join me at the lake today?"

Her cheeks warmed and her insides filled with fritterflies. Her mind replayed a few of her recent stolen moments at the nearby Lake Neev with Zephner. "No," she said. "I have to find Elloise. Have you seen her?"

He shook his head. "Where did you last see her?"

"I haven't seen her today." She couldn't mention being a Caretaker or that she was looking for more than Elloise—even though she wanted to. "Muriel asked me to find Elloise."

"I could help."

"But you were heading to the lake…"

"Yeah, to escape more lessons and my mother telling me to stand straighter." A mischievous glint filled his chocolate-colored eyes. "I can do that while helping you find Lady El."

"Okay." Acna's mind fell back on something the Crown Prince had told her a few weeks ago. When he and his sister were little the queen had a horrible time keeping nannies. The only person to get along with the headstrong queen and her children was Elloise. So, to keep the whispers about her servant caring for her children away, Queen Impora raised Elloise from a servant of the house to a lady. But the fancy title never kept Elloise from the hard work she enjoyed.

"I can search the west wing," said Zephner.

"Then I'll look in the east wing."

"How about we meet back here when we're done?"

"But how will we alert each other if one has found Elloise?"

He tickled the leaf of a flower. "I have a Talent with plants, remember?"

She nodded.

"If I've found her, I'll have the plants waving. If you find Elloise let a plant know and they'll tell me. Then we can come back to the fruit tree."

Acna smiled. "I can handle that."

The two friends parted ways.

Acna had scoured both lower levels of the palace. She secretly hoped the missing book and Elloise would be on the main floor in the queen's study or the ballroom—or maybe the lobby. If not, the second floor where the servants lived, and the guest quarters were kept was a good place. But the old woman wasn't on either floor. Acna twisted the long ties of her apron. She really didn't want to go up to the third floor where the royal family lived and slept. But she couldn't see a way around it.

She climbed the curving staircase to the circular third floor. The landing was an open area with doors to various rooms and a few alcoves with large windows surrounding it. The small space felt like a home. Set in an alcove was a round breakfast table and some chairs. The open door to one of the rooms revealed the royal children's study area. The tutor, Master Dumor, was asleep at his post. Acna knew that the bedrooms of the queen and the two royal siblings were located on this floor, too. She wasn't sure what lay behind the rest of the doors.

She started with the first door to her left and worked her way around. She discovered a nursery, two spare bedrooms, a storage area, and an empty room beyond what she thought was there. Searching the prince's room had felt wrong—he was her friend and she'd not been invited into his space—but she needed to find Elloise. Unfortunately, there was no sign of the woman.

Acna entered the classroom and rang the bell on Master Dumor's desk.

The teacher opened his emerald-green eyes and yawned. His caramel-colored fists raised high above his gray-haired head as he stretched. "Hello, Acna."

"Hello, Master Dumor," she said as something purple shimmered to her right. "I was wondering if you've seen Lady Elloise today." Her heart rate slowly increased. Had she found the book?

"No." He got up from his chair. "There's a wonderful smell in the air. Is my wife at work on lunch already?"

"Most likely dinner, sir. The lunch hour is long past."

"Well, I'd best see if there are leftovers since neither of the queen's children are present for their lessons anyway." He headed for the door. "I wish you luck on finding Elloise. The woman is better at hiding than a mythic Vinchett."

"Yes ... sir."

He left.

Sitting atop a purple book was an amethyst-colored, eight-legged insect known as a Vinchett. Its leaf-green eyes glittered in the sunlight.

Relief cascaded through Acna's tense muscles. "You."

The bug twitched an antenna.

"I should have known that wherever the Treaty volume landed you would be there."

Another twitch.

"Where's Elloise?" The tension in her stomach returned.

The insect lifted the hard shells that covered its delicate wings like it was shrugging, admitting it had no clue where the old Grigorian woman was. Then it flew onto a shelf.

Acna crossed the room and picked up the book. She would resume her hunt for Elloise after dealing with the magical tome. She scanned the study. "We can't leave this here. It's too open. Besides, Master Dumor may see its seemingly empty pages and have one of his charges write in it."

She rubbed her fingers along the soft leather of the plum-colored book. Her mind reviewed the various places she had been. Where could she temporarily hide the volume until Muriel could deal with it properly? Her breath caught.

She hurried from the study and into the spare room with the cream-white canopy over the stone framed bed. In the corner by the doors for the balcony was a bookshelf. She crossed to it and slipped the Treaty book between two larger tomes. There, it was safe for a moment.

The Vinchett crawled across the bedroom floor and hopped onto the bookshelf. Then, it wedged itself behind the books.

The high branches of a fruit tree waved. Acna carefully opened the glass doors onto the balcony and examined the garden. Below the tree stood Prince Zephner and Lady Elloise. "Thank the Creator," she whispered. There wasn't a plant close enough to inform she saw the prince, so she left the balcony, closed the doors, and exited the bedroom.

In the lobby Acna found Muriel. She notified the older servant of Elloise's whereabouts and the current placement of the Treaty volume. Muriel thanked Acna for her hard work before Acna went for the garden.

She smiled as she spied her friends beneath the fruit tree. Each had a bumpy oval fruit known as a pordy. The fruit's reddish liquid dripped from their faces and hands.

Elloise raised her snack. "It's ripe enough for Cook's tarts! Master Dumor is surely licking his chops."

"Yup." Acna plucked a ripened fruit from a low limb on the tree. She'd eaten lunch before her short nap but was hungry from searching the palace.

Elloise tossed the stem of her treat into the bushes. "You two youngsters make a cute couple." She sucked the juice from her wrinkled hands. "It will be grand to see what you do together when you grow up."

Heat seared Acna's face. She liked Zephner, they'd been friends for years, and thoughts of being more had started to fill her head, but for Elloise to blatantly say what she thought was crazy.

Pink tinged the prince's dark cheeks. He chuckled. "Do you know something we don't, Lady El?"

A breeze played with the white wisps of Elloise's hair as she smirked. "I know many things you two don't."

GLOW IN THE DARK

By Allyn Schuyler

My mother knelt beside my bed
As was her nightly rite,
She brushed my hair back from my head
And kissed me sweet goodnight.

Well, I was such a cheeky boy
And dearly loved to play,
So, I pressed my hand into a fist
To scrub that kiss away.

Oh no, said my dear mother
You can't rub away that mark!
Why, I still see it sitting there
Brightly glowing in the dark.

You see, a mother's kiss never fades
And it never goes away,
It doesn't matter how you try
It will stay with you till someday…

That kiss will put a smile
Back on your face and in your heart.
And one day when you're older
And when we are far apart,

Those kisses will remind you
And bring back to memory,
All the happy times and love we shared
Within our family.

And on those cold and rainy days
That always seem to come,
Those kisses will be glowing
And will warm you, like the sun.

So, don't even try to rub away
Your mother's precious kiss,
'Cause it will bring back memories
That you won't want to miss.

And it, with all the ones before
Will help you find your way,
When you are lost and wondering
Which way to go someday.

And if you ever feel as though
No one seems to care,
Just come back home for another kiss
I will always have a spare.

Well, many years have come and gone
And what Mother said was true,
I still can feel her kisses
And her love come shining through.

Yes, time has passed, but one thing
The years did not erase,
Are the kisses that my mother shared
With love, in her embrace.

Baron and the New Beginning

By Peggy Bodde

Baron was staring out the car window and didn't even realize he was biting his fingernails until his mom said, "Baron! Stop biting your nails. And we're here. We're at your new school."

Baron didn't move except to push his hair to the side, so it wasn't hanging in his eyes. He stared at all the new faces and the tall gray building and sighed.

He and his mom had already visited the school, but it looked a lot scarier and bigger now. He looked at the swarm of strangers and felt sick to his stomach. Even though fall was his favorite season, the bright orange and yellow trees around the school were painful reminders of the friends he'd left behind.

His mom turned around from the driver's seat. "Come on, honey. You'll make new friends. It'll be fun."

Baron slowly opened the car door and stepped out onto the sidewalk, adjusting his backpack. His mom leaned over to smile at him through the passenger window. "Bye! Have a great day!"

Baron looked at his mom and waved one hand as he slowly walked in the direction of the classroom. He could feel himself frowning and dragging his feet as he thought about the past few months.

Baron had spent his whole life in Tennessee. All ten years of it. Usually in October, he and his friends went to the fall festival at church. They also got together at someone's house, carved pumpkins, and ate chilidogs. It was a tradition.

But in August, Baron's dad had gotten a new job. His parents explained that a "promotion" was a great thing. It meant that his dad was moving up in the company, but it also meant that the family would have to move to Utah in October. Utah was far away from Tennessee. If they drove without stopping, it would take all day and all night to get there: twenty-four hours.

"And, here we are," Baron said to himself. He walked into the classroom and felt everyone's eyes on him. His hands felt sweaty when he realized that the only open seat was in the front row. He didn't look at anyone and sat down as fast as he could. He was in such a hurry that he forgot to take off his backpack, which got wedged in the seat. He stood up and heard some laughter. His face turned bright red as he slipped off the backpack and sat down again.

The teacher, Mrs. Hamilton, was friendly and full of energy as she walked around the classroom and talked to all the students. She introduced Baron, but she didn't make him stand up in front of the class, which was a relief. The rest of the morning went by in a blur. Soon, it was lunchtime, and Baron wasn't looking forward to sitting by himself. All the students rushed out to the cafeteria, but he took his time.

Mrs. Hamilton smiled and asked, "Are you all set for lunch, Baron? I know it can be difficult to start over at a new school."

"Yes ma'am. Thank you." Baron had noticed that people in Utah didn't say "sir" and "ma'am" which seemed strange to him. "One more way that things are different here," he thought.

He turned to go and saw another student who was also lagging behind. Baron couldn't help but notice that the boy was extremely short. He was much shorter than any ten-year old Baron had ever met. The boy dropped a book he had been trying to push into his bulging backpack. It hit the floor with a loud smack.

"I'll get that," Baron said. He grabbed the book and held it out. The boy smiled and thanked him.

He crammed the book into his backpack and asked, "Your name's Baron, right? Where'd you move from?"

Baron was surprised the boy remembered his name. "Um. That's right. I'm Baron. I moved from Tennessee. What's your name?"

"Landon. Great to meet you, Baron."

Landon was friendly and easy to talk to. He invited Baron to eat lunch with him. As the two boys walked to the cafeteria, Baron noticed that Landon could do everything Baron could do. Landon was just shorter. After they got their food and sat down, Landon looked up and said, "Are you curious? About my height?"

"Yes. I mean, I've just never met anyone..."

"It's ok, Baron! Really. I have something called dwarfism. It means I'll always be shorter than everyone else, but I can pretty much do anything I want. Except basketball." Landon grinned. "I don't think I'll ever be much of a basketball player."

Baron laughed. A couple more students who knew Landon came and sat down at the table, and Landon introduced them to Baron. The rest of the day went much better. Baron was excited to tell his parents about Landon and his other new friends.

At dinner that night, Baron said, 'Landon is so positive and happy, Dad. And he introduced me to his other friends. And he told me a lot about dwarfism. I'd never even heard of it before. And he doesn't mind when people ask questions, and…"

"Whoa! Slow down, son. He sounds like a great person. I'm glad you met him."

"Me too, Dad. Maybe he can come over some time."

Later, Baron was lying in bed and thinking that Utah may not be so bad after all when his parents came in to say goodnight.

"You remember when we prayed about my new school and making friends?" Baron asked.

"Of course," his mom answered.

"Well, when I first saw Landon, I thought maybe God wanted me to be his friend because he was different, and he needed a friend. But it turns out that I'm the one who needed him."

Baron's parents hugged him and said goodnight. After they left, he said a little prayer of thanks for Landon and fell asleep with a smile on his face.

OCTOBER

By Neal Johnson

The wind fought its way across the dry October ground.
It picked its way through the dusty, dying grass
And curled around the feet of those standing by.
Hair bounced playfully on bowed heads.
Skirts and trousers buffeted back and forth
With the tide of the wind.

Leaves rolled over themselves
As barren trees beckoned the wind on.
Hands unconsciously moved
To cover the restless cloth;
And feet silently stirred
To avoid the restive leaves.

And somewhere,
Somewhere through that solitude
That seemed only to be broken
By the wind and its burdens,
Somewhere over the hum of occasional wasps
Seeking the flowers scattered on the ground,

Somewhere through this busy silence
A voice could sometimes be heard.
It spoke in familiar tones and phrases.
Words of the Apostle Paul,
Words of the risen Christ,
Words about the comfort after death.

Each person, from his own small plot of ground,
Stood in silence and listened.
Sometimes to the wind and the leaves,
Sometimes to the minister and his words,
Sometimes to his own mind and fears,
Searching for something else to think about.

The day was cold
But the sun offered warmth.
It beat down on the faces
Of those whose heads were not bowed.
It gently stung the lips of the silent
And caressed their bodies in ways no lover could.

It spoke of life and proffered a shield
Against the coldness of the wind
And the pain of the moment.
It gave reprieve to those standing by
And a note of nostalgia for those seated
By the opening in the ground.

The words ceased.
The muffled sobbing of bereaved women caught the wind
And, for a moment—a very slight moment—hung there.
Chairs rustled and were emptied.
People slowly moved away:
Some too soon to return.

The wind danced where the people had stood.
The leaves chattered
Where there had only been silence.
And the sun, like the people,
Tired from a long day of too little warmth,
Began to seek a resting place.

Only darkness remained
In the freshly turned burial ground.
Only darkness, with its dead Fall leaves,
It's now stilled wind
And its newest resident,
Remained to see the night through.

Each of the four, in their own way, died this cold October day,
Yet only one of them is now capable
Of answering the eternal question
That has plagued humanity throughout time.
Only one of these can now bear witness for us
To the eternal mystery of life's true ending.

Neither the wind, leaves, darkness nor silenced man,
None, but one, can now solve the unsolvable riddle.
Only one can now lift the veil of death for us to see.
But in his new reality, he is forever restrained to leave us sightless,
With only our fears, our faith and our hope
To prepare us for our own cold October day.

COASTING OR COMPETING?

By Gregg Heid

I enjoy riding my bike with a tail wind or coasting down hills. I fly down a path effortlessly with no peddling. I can stand on the pedals as I look around and stretch my legs with the wind in my face. But riding into a headwind or up a hill is a chore.

When I ride against the wind, my nose runs, and I breathe hard. My arms tire and my neck stiffens. When I pedal up-hill I feel pain in my thighs and calves.

So, why do athletes challenge hills and confront the winds? Because both build muscles and increase stamina.

Though most of us are not athletic competitors, we're all participants in the race the Apostle Paul writes about in his first letter to the Corinthians (9:24-27 NASB). *"We are training to win the race set before us. Everyone who competes in the games, exercises self-control in all things. I discipline my body and make it my slave. I run in such a way, as not without aim; I box in such a way, as not beating the air."*

Paul is not talking about getting in physical shape. He says to Timothy, *"Bodily discipline is of little profit, but godliness is profitable for all things since it holds promise for the present life and also for the life to come."* (1Timothy 4:8 NASB)

Paul suffered years in prison, rejection and persecution by society, and worked to exhaustion to spread the gospel. The early church fathers state that he was beheaded by the Romans after he returned from his fifth missionary journey.

So, why was he competing if death was his end? Because Paul knew death wasn't his end, but—as a follower of Christ—his translation into

God's glory with the imperishable *crown* of righteousness (2 Timothy.4:8). This crown puts him in the winner's circle with the saints in heaven.

Are you coasting: going with the flow of the world, or running uphill after Christ?

STAR SONG

By Blythe McHatton

Once a bright, shining star shone in the cosmos. Red-brown rays surrounded her crown. She observed her world through orbs that matched the rays in uncanny, sometimes mystifying ways. Happiness filled her life. Though she experienced trials and sorrows, the depth of them rarely ran deep.

Around this star, others were usually laughing, or at least smiling, for she brought joy into every life she brushed—even casually. In her, others found warmth. From her, they received love. She was funny. She drew them like a flame. Others were compelled to be around her.

But as in all stories, this star–

In her compassionate, caring heart, another's trouble overwhelmed her. The problem started when, in doing so, she allowed a fissure in her armor.

Now a crack in any warrior's armor is sensed by a foe. In this case, however, her adversary needed little skill at detecting weakness. Her strong inner light streaked from the thin slit with a glowing brilliance that drew Enemy from half a world away. He wasted no time, but with great relish took up the battle in the form of a pack of ravenous hyenas.

Pride said to Hate and Lust, "Let me run the first leg of the chase. I'll start her downfall. "

The others quickly agreed.

"Aren't you glad you are a better wife than she is?" Pride whispered in Star's ear. "You would never treat Beloved like that. And the little ones—how could anyone neglect her offspring in such a callous manner."

Deceiver came to join in the fun. Clever, he never spoke to Star directly. He used the Friend's voice. "You are wonderful, Star. So understanding. So kind. I don't know how I would solve my problems without you."

She knew better. She recognized flattery when she heard it. Still, she couldn't resist the flutter of pleasure at hearing praise, something missing from her Beloved recently. The result made her try harder to help. Surely Creator would be pleased with her effort.

Hate picked up where Pride left off. "How could anyone treat Friend that way?" he asked Star. "He is so hurt. Only someone evil would be so unkind, uncaring, selfish." The ploy didn't take long. He planted a clue here and spoke a word in her ear there.

All the while, Deceiver played his part. "You are beautiful," he said through Friend. "My day is full when you are here for me, here to help me."

Hate continued to justify himself. She believed his lies.

On and on, the grisly throng wove their ugly play with Star at center stage. She took on the role and played it to the fullest. If Deceiver spurred Friend to suggest the need for Star to demonstrate her concern for him by touching him, she did. If he hinted she be aggressive and prove he was attractive to her, she performed. She convinced herself Creator would be pleased.

She managed to maintain the pretense until the day she crossed the line. That day she completed her betrayal of Friend's wife and children, of her Beloved, of herself, and of most importance – she betrayed Creator. She didn't do it without conscious thought. She had simply come to a time when Deceiver's words rang truer and more important to her than Creator's.

Such a sad day.

———— ❧ ————

Though Star thought all was lost, it was not.

Creator does not give up His own easily. Even as Star remained immersed in the betrayal day after day, Creator had His own plan. He whispered to Beloved in dreams and in waking hours. Creator opened the eyes of those around Star who loved her and trusted her too much to believe what they saw her doing. He used those who loved Him to challenge the lies Star told herself were truth.

Finally, Creator loosed Conviction to speak to Star.

Battles of such magnitude are never easily won, not even when the Creator of all the Universe is in the midst. However, there is never doubt as to who will win in the end, not when the one involved loves Creator as much as Star did. The haze of self-indulgence can overwhelm that love for a time, but it cannot conquer in the final moments.

And it didn't.

She pulled her misdirected thoughts to a halt. "Star," she said to herself, "you are hearing lies. Believing them has led you to grievously hurt Beloved whom you care for only slightly less than Creator."

It became Despair's turn to chase Star over the plains. "No hope for you. You ruined your life. You ruined Beloved's life and your children's lives. Creator will never take you back."

For a moment, Star believed Despair. For a moment, she considered putting out her light and becoming a black hole in the universe.

Fortunately, before taking such a drastic step she cried, "Creator, I've done so much wrong. Gone my own way. Is there no hope for me?"

Throughout the universe, silence reigned – the silence of all waiting for His answer.

"I love you," came the still small voice.

Tears dampened her cheeks. The breath she'd held in check for weeks spewed. She stood mute for a long time before she could ask, "Oh, Creator, can you still love me? I have been ugly, so ugly, and have caused too much harm."

"I love you," He said again.

Star drew a deep clean breath and valiantly ignored all the words Fear shrieked in her ear. In that moment, she stood resolute, face toward Creator, and accepted His Truth.

"I love you," the words echoed yet a third time.

"I believe you," she answered at last. "I love you. With my whole heart, I love you.

"Yes," Creator said, "You do."

"Please forgive me."

"It is done."

"Everything will be all right?"

"In the end. It will never be as it might have been, and there will be pain. But in the end, my Star, everything will be all right."

Don't Do It

By Jesse Wenzel

My off-ramp came in sight as I drove home from the late shift at an Atlantic City casino. Exiting before me was a beat-up, 1950s-something pickup. As if about to expire, the driver slowed down from an absurd 15 miles an hour to a ridiculous 5. I'd have needed to be parked not to tailgate him. In response, the driver nearly stopped. I quickly went around him on the right, accelerated onto the median grass, and cut back in front of him.

My aggressive move jump-started his adrenaline. He put on his high beams and rode my bumper. *Screw you*, I said to myself. A sharper voice inside my head knew my next move and cried out, "Don't do it!" But I gave the one-finger salute out my window anyway. *What's an old fart gonna do about it?*

I stopped at the end of the ramp, turned right, and sped a quarter-mile to the next traffic signal. As I sat in the right turn lane, "Old fart" pulled up behind me. After this turn, it was a mile-and-a-half to my next exit. I knew I'd outdistance him on the straightaway.

After making the turn, I floored my 4-door Honda Civic. A mile down the road, it was as if I was pulling a trailer that looked like a truck! To shake my tail, I decided to feign going straight and make a quick right instead. And though I did my part, the pickup never left me.

In the movie, *Butch Cassidy & The Sundance Kid*, when Butch and Sundance are unable to outfox the Pinkerton agents tracking them, one looks at the other and says, "Who are these guys?" In the same way, the old truck driven by some old guy made me wonder, *Who is this guy?*

I'd had my fun back on the ramp. *Why is he taking things so seriously?* Our "moment" should have ended back then. *Maybe I should pull over and we can talk things out.* To which I again heard, "Don't do it!"

A mile from my driveway, I hoped his adrenaline was wearing off. He had to know he was freaking me out, as I was driving as fast as my 4-cylinders would go.

Approaching my dark driveway, I heard anew, "Don't do it!" And I knew not to pull into my drive. So, I sped past to a stop sign two-hundred feet away, made a fast right to another traffic light and, without stopping, took another right onto a straightaway.

On that stretch the old guy pulled into the passing lane to come alongside me. *What's he going to do, run me off the road?* His old beat-up truck could have slammed into my car without adding a scratch to his. "Stop!" I heard that same voice and shoved my brake pedal to the floor. I backed around and headed to the nearest town three miles away. He hadn't expected my move, as I put some distance between us.

I ran a red light and made a left back the way I'd come. Very soon we were re-attached as one. But I sensed he wasn't as upset as before, as we were now going through the motions doing 60 mph, not 90. His anger had apparently changed from seeing me as his prey to, "I can do this all night long."

He could have turned around and gone home without losing face. And when he'd tell the story he'd be justified in saying, "Yeah, I bet that guy stopped at WAWA for diapers before he went home."

As my emotions settled and my head cleared, a light came on. *I'll head to the police station. That should scare him off.*

I soon pulled into the police parking lot, under a street lamp next to the sidewalk that lead into the station. Fortunately, a policeman was walking towards me to his car. He looked in my direction just as the old truck came to an abrupt halt next to my car.

I got out and stood inside my opened door. The truck driver did the same.

Puzzled, the cop asked us, "Is everything OK?" Before either of us could answer he spoke again, "Hey, Dave. Is that you?"

What! You know this psycho?

Dave looked at me as I stared back at him. He then spoke for the both of us. "Yeah, it's me, Tom. Everything's OK."

Tom got in his patrol car and drove off.

At least now I have a credible witness if I turn up dead.

The "old guy," 20-years my younger, took charge. "You have children?"

What? Are you some kind of counselor? But instead of sharing my thoughts I answered, "Yeah, two young girls."

"You're an idiot."

Before I could respond Dave finished, "You almost got shot tonight."

What? I could see that my best move was not to make one.

So, Dave, our new-group leader asked, "You drink?"

"Not much."

"You want to get a drink?" Which was not a question but a statement.

"Sure." Whatever it took to get this nut in my corner I thought it best to do.

Dave pointed across the street to an all-night bar that cops frequented. "I'll meet you over there."

Dave waited for me as I got out of my car and we silently walked in together. There were seven customers and a bartender inside. Each looked up and said, "Hi, Dave."

Who is this guy?

We sat at the bar and Dave did most of the talking. About five years ago he was a rookie cop in this town. On a traffic stop he was doing a test on a drunk driver when the driver's inebriated girlfriend came up behind Dave and hit him in the head with her shoe. He reacted by punching her in the face, then beating up the boyfriend who came to her aide. Dave was kicked off the force.

Dave moved to Florida and worked construction. He broke up with his girlfriend and told his roommate—a friend of hers—not to date his ex. Anything but that. Weeks later he caught them in bed together and shot his roommate in the leg! But because Dave had the "goods" on his "old buddy," his roommate didn't press charges. Dave returned to New Jersey and was now sitting with me in the bar.

Six months and a day ago he'd been convicted of drunk driving. This night, our night, was the first time he'd (legally) driven since getting back his license. He told me if I'd flipped him the bird the night before, he'd have gone home rather chase after me; afraid of losing his license permanently.

With a few drinks in us we were now buddies. It was like I was his old roommate and we were laughing about the "glory days" when he'd shot me in the leg.

I told him I'd thought of pulling over and talking things out, to which Dave said, "I'd have shot *you* in the leg."

What? Really? I laughed because I was nervous again. *Who is this guy?*

Then Dave offered, "I pulled up alongside you to shoot into your car. But my passenger window was up so I didn't."

Dave's last bit of advice was to tell me the best thing I'd done was to drive to the police station. "Other than that," he said, "you're a complete idiot." He smirked as he raised his glass to his mouth.

I'd had enough to drink, and a lot to mull over. I pulled out my wallet, which Dave waved off, "I got it," as we parted ways.

More than "tipsy," I was a half-mile from home when I got pulled over by flashing lights. *What a night! And I don't even drink.*

It was Dave's buddy, Officer Tom.

Tom recognized me from two hours earlier, "You're Dave's buddy, right?"

"Yes." I thought to myself, *Tonight, we're all buddies.*

"This is your lucky night."

I gagged as I laughed out loud. Tom excused my response as that of a drunk.

"You live nearby?"

"Just up the street."

"Can you drive without knocking things over?"

"Sure."

"I'll follow you until you pull into your drive. Promise me you won't go out again tonight."

"Not a chance."

The next day I woke up, knowing it hadn't been a dream. I needed to pick up my daughters from their mom's at noon. When my ex crossed my mind I thought, *She thinks I'm an idiot, too.* I called her to confirm and was tempted to share my bizarre story; as I had to tell someone. The voice in my head returned, "Don't do it! If you do, you really are an idiot."

I never saw Dave again. With his moxie, he's probably a successful and corrupt politician.

Is this how God gets through to those who won't otherwise listen to Him? Precisely. In hindsight, our lives leak clues like a car needing maintenance. And when we won't heed the Master Mechanic's voice, make sure you're wearing your seatbelt.

REDEMPTION

By Peggy Bodde

Broken Heart of Gethsemane,
betrayal's sorrow
known by God,
felt by man.
The kiss of death,
The Bread of Life.

The Covenant spills warm
as darkness pounds
the jagged spikes,
embraced by outstretched arms
and open hands,
a weeping side.

Cold, shiny coins
flung carelessly
by the wicked
blindly smack the Cross and

as they fall—
their reflection captures
the sinner's face,
my own.

A Fragile Heart

By April Adamson Holthaus

My tourist gene kicked in as my plane landed at the Vienna airport that June day. In true tourist style, I learned train schedules, brought the perfect walking shoes, and poured over guidebooks. A world traveler since childhood, I've adapted to many cultures. *Wow, six months in Europe. Think of all the history here. I've got this!*

It turned out I'd forgotten to prepare for loneliness and insecurity. The recent death of my husband left me struggling for self-worth and value. The title "widow" didn't fit.

I thought I'd try something new when I volunteered for a non-profit organization headquartered near Baden, Austria. This six-month stay was to help organize their November publisher's conference in Moscow. The excitement of travel erased any initial cautions. I expected positive things from this arrangement.

At first, new customs in Austria took some adjustment. In the past, I never felt like an outsider when I traveled with my husband. Now a part-time resident in Baden, I needed to strictly observe cultural nuances. To fit in, a less casual look was required. The residents were reserved but polite, not quite friendly. The Austrian greeting, *Gruss Gott*, was to be spoken on entering a shop or open market to elicit any service. I felt out of place.

To remain in Austria past the thirty-day visa required registration at the town hall. A local bank account was needed for direct deposits. With my presence registered and funds secured to assure payment of my rent, phone, and food, I requested a telephone. It was my lifeline for AOL dial-up.

I rented a large room with a small kitchen and bath eight blocks from town center. It had basic pieces of furniture and a large window with wonderful light. The rent was high. My hot water was on a twenty-minute timer. My transportation was on the end of my legs. Whatever I wanted to transport to my little space was restricted to what fit in my backpack, very different from loading up a car in Colorado.

Living in Baden posed challenges and though I tried to adapt day after day, I felt more the lonely outsider. Inconveniences, like walking everywhere in the summer heat, made me peevish. I selfishly thought others should reach out to me. I walked around as if in a bubble where people couldn't see me.

My daily commute to our office began with a six-block walk to the Tram office to purchase my ticket, then a twenty-minute ride on the little commuter train, and finally another long walk. I rehearsed short German phrases to pass the time as I observed small vineyards on the slopes.

I began to doubt my reasons for staying. Unappreciated for my efforts at the office, a sense of incompetence nearly defeated me as I endured "helpful" criticism. Crushed, I inwardly railed against the price of volunteering. I submerged my frustration with a mental growl and took directions without arguing. I could have seen Europe for what it cost me to stay and deal with perceived put-downs every day. On weekends, my reprieve was to lose the hurts and travel by train to Prague or Budapest.

Then my struggles increased. Renters in my Colorado condo broke the lease and moved, compromising my resources. This setback tested my resolve. I wasn't a quitter. I choked out a prayer for wisdom.

Tired from each day's negativity and long walks, I climbed the stairs to my room, fixed a simple meal and ate—alone. I looked forward to working on my laptop to connect me with friends and family back home. I used dial-up internet to connect to my AOL account, quickly downloaded messages, then shut down the connection to save money. Notes of encouragement over the internet fed my lonely heart. I felt loved. I unburdened my soul in lengthy messages, dialed into AOL, and hit *Send*.

I hadn't anticipated grief and loneliness to be heightened by the solitude I experienced on a daily basis. I lived alone. I traveled alone. I missed my husband. Tears came often without reason. There was no interested somebody to occasionally share new experiences. There was an uncomfortable reality of not belonging, and when you don't, those feelings are heightened. I resisted crawling into a protective bubble.

Pervasive feelings of loneliness went underground during the day but were foremost in my heart at night. I passed long evenings immersed in stories of the Hapsburgs of Austria to bury and cancel those thoughts.

Finally tired, I clicked off the light, snuggled under a fluffy duvet, prayed for peace of heart, and fell asleep.

Soon new doors opened. My Austrian landlady invited me to tea and German lessons one hour a week. As I learned numbers, names of items, and idioms, a connection to the community opened. I used *bitte*, please, and *danke*, thank you, more often. When I met someone I said, *guten tag*, good day. I could negotiate prices!

I smiled at strangers and didn't need a positive response. I met four American girls also living in Baden. Movie night at their place was a treat. Another new friend offered a ride to the large market and delivered me home with heavy bags. These small kindnesses and interactions removed some of the heartache of widowhood. I began to relax and feel a part of the community.

In late July our director invited me to accompany her to Singapore, Beijing, and then Hong Kong, a three-week trip. What gracious Christian publishers we met. New cities, new cultures, and God's people halfway around the world! My appetite for travel was appeased.

Returning to our office in Austria, we continued to prepare for the three-week conference outside Moscow in November. Russian publishers came from Moldavia, Belarus, Ukraine, and Siberia. They traveled by train and bus, some for two or three days. It was a privilege to serve them. They were dedicated to excellence in their publications to share the gospel with their people.

Part of my routine was to forage for teatime goodies for the conference staff. With three layers under my ankle-length down coat, a hat covering all but my frozen nose, and three pairs of socks in my fur-lined boots, I had never been so cold. Mid-November was minus twenty degrees or so!

I walked a mile round-trip to outdoor stalls to fill my wheeled bag with candy bars, cookies, and sodas. In the stalls, Pampers were displayed next to ladies' bras and varieties of bakery items. Frozen fish were slammed onto the solid concrete to break them into the size customers wanted. It was an experience indelibly seared in my memory.

As I returned home in December I knew God had given me hope for a new future. He'd used grief, solitude, fear, and insecurities from this experience to strengthen my fragile heart. He showed me I had purpose. I'd stuck with hard things and experienced life in new ways. I had fun, met new people, and learned to trust Him.

SILENCE

By Neal Johnson

Silence is here.
And what a strange companion she is.
She is a temperamental mistress
Here to mirror my fears and my doubts,
Here to satisfy my longings.

She is all I desire at one moment
All I abhor the next.
She can be soothing or hard,
Loving or cruel,
Flamboyant or moody.

She can be noisy and feared and hated.
She can be peace and meditation and rest.
She can intimidate, and she can sustain.

She is like the people who hear her.
She is the people who hear her.

DT

By Gregg Heid

Back in seventh grade my nemesis moved to town. I was walking to my cousin's house when I went by his yard and his two chow-collie crosses charged out after me. I thought about running but they were too fast, so I let go with a kick that caught the first one under the chin and sent him over backwards. The second grabbed my pant cuff and was yanking my leg back and forth when I heard, "Get over here." Both dogs ran back to a stocky kid with big arms and a cigarette in his mouth. "What the hell you doin kickin one of my dogs?"

"He attacked me. Keep em in your yard or tie em up."

"It's a free country, and my dogs like to be free, so you can walk another street."

As I sized him up, I thought…maybe I can take him, but he looks tough. "I like this street so keep em tied or I'll bring a stick next time."

"And I'll kick your ass."

"Try it." I just finished the sentence and he hit me square in the face.

I wrestled in sixth grade, so I went for his legs and took him down. We rolled around on the gravel and threw punches when we could. After a couple minutes we were both too tired to go on. Smoking didn't help his wind and I was glad to quit.

"Time out," he gasped. "I need a cig. Want one?"

That was his peace offering. So, I took my first cigarette from the new kid in town. "Sure."

He lit his, replaced it with another, then used the first one to light mine and handed it to me.

"What's your name?" I asked.

"Danny, Danny Thistle. My friends where I came from called me DT for 'Damn Tough.'"

From then on, I felt kinda special cuz I knew this new kid in school. He wore T-shirts with his camels rolled up in the sleeve and he cussed like a miner after a day underground. But we also had this friction between us. Deep down we didn't like each other, but we tolerated each other. Everything we did became a competition that turned into a daring contest.

After school one day, he dared me first. "Heid, bet you can't do this." He dropped a daddy long-leg into his mouth and swallowed it whole.

I followed suit by finding the smallest one I could find on the school's concrete foundation. I gagged but kept it down.

The next time he upped the ante. "Bet you're too chicken to do this." He ducked under the three-rail fence and ran out into the middle of the field where Thompson's Angus bull stared at him. He picked up a rock and threw it. The bull put his head down, pawed the ground with his front hoof and threw dirt onto his back. Then he charged full speed. DT ran for his life and ducked under the wood rail fence five feet ahead of the bull. The 1500-pound animal couldn't stop in time and hit the fence, knocking off the top rail. I jumped back as his bulging eyes glared at me and the snot flew from his nose.

Mr. Thompson rode up on his horse, chewed us out for harassing his bull and made us put back the rail on the fence. "You boys get on outta here."

Thank you, Jesus. I didn't have to follow through with my end of the dare.

The next week was my turn. I swam at the public pool all summer, so I dared him to swim across the Yampa River. I went first and ended up crossing 20 yards downstream because of the strong current.

He hesitated for a minute and I thought I'd won. Nope, he dove in head first and swam like a baby duck trying to keep up with its mother; arms slapping the water and his head turning side to side with each stroke. What he lacked in technique he made up for in determination. Finally, he made it across, 30 yards below me, cussing and spitting water as he gasped for air on the river bank.

I now had the upper hand and he knew it. So, the last week of school he led me over to the railroad tracks by the rodeo grounds.

"What are we doing over here?" I said.

"You'll see." He stood quietly throwing pebbles at a discarded Coors can.

Five minutes passed, then ten. "This is boring," I said. "Let's go." Then we heard the train coming from the West. As I watched the engine grow, I wondered what Danny Thistle had up his sleeve. I soon found out.

When the train was an eighth of a mile from us, he yelled, "You're too chicken for this." He ran onto the tracks and laid down between the rails. The entire train passed over him as he laid like a corpse for five minutes. When the caboose went by, he jumped up and said, "Your turn next."

"No way, you're crazy." I walked away and never saw DT again. They moved to another town that summer, not far away. I heard later that he was in reform school.

I did one more dare after Danny. Eight years later I met an atheist at college. She told me she couldn't believe in a god who allowed so much poverty, war, suffering and sorrow on planet earth. All my arguments and apologetics failed to convince her that God is not the author of sin and suffering but that He always makes something good come from it.

So, I dared her to give God a chance. "Being an atheist is having faith in no god," I said. "Give Him a month, what can it hurt? Ask Him to reveal Himself to you. If nothing happens, you're still an atheist with your same beliefs. You lose nothing. If you do encounter Him, you win."

She's now a nun with the Carmelite Sisters of The Divine Heart of Jesus.

SATURDAY

by Lynn Moffett

"Isn't it ... good ... out here?"

"Yes, Dad, it's a beautiful day."

As we cruise along the Foothill Freeway, the mountains loom upward, velvet tan dotted with dark green oaks. The sky is the sharp blue of fall with an occasional white cloud wisping overhead. But even had it been smoggy and breathlessly hot, Dad would have said, "Isn't it ... good ... out here?" and I would have replied, "Yes, it is a beautiful day."

His hand pats mine where it rests on the console between our seats. I reach up and catch his as he withdraws, reminded he is a man who draws life from the touch of a hand, a man with a tremendous need for reassurance these days.

I say, "The mountains are vivid against the sky. Remember how in spring they are plush green with patches of poppies, lupine, and mustard?"

He nods. "That one, that one."

"Uh-huh, that's the Green Hill." This is our term for Mission Peak which sits watch above Dad's house, a house he no longer inhabits.

He nods again.

I squeeze his hand. "And then, as spring grows old, they turn brown as quickly as eastern fall trees change from green to a Van Gogh painting to bare."

"Isn't it ... good ... out here?" Changing the subject, he says, "Have you seen Bill?"

"No, haven't even talked with him this week on the phone."

We cruise a few more miles. "Isn't it ... good ... out here?"

"Yes, Dad, a beautiful day."

"Have you seen Bill?'

"No. I haven't. Have you seen him?"

"Who?"

"Bill."

"Bill?'

"Your son, Dad. Have you seen Bill?'

He looks bewildered.

I say, "That big guy you love, who lives in your house."

"Big guy? My house? Oh. Is his name Bill? I love him."

"Did he take you to the doctor Wednesday?"

"The doctor? I don't—"

"Didn't Bill take you to get your blood tested?"

Dad motions to his forearm vein and says, "Here."

"Yes, Daddy. Your blood. Did Bill take you for your blood test?"

"Yes, I think ... went up and there and did that." As he says these words, his hands are miming them, but comprehension eludes me. We sit in silence, hands once again touching.

After a few more miles I ask, "Did you go to the house? Work on the house?"

"No. Yes. I don't ... Isn't it ... good ... out here?"

"Yes, Daddy, it's a beautiful day."

By now we are approaching the Osborne off-ramp, not our destination, but one we used to take us to church each Sunday during the months of freeway earthquake cleanup and reconstruction. At that time, we were both singing in the choir. Months have passed since. Dad has deteriorated to the degree that we moved him into an environment that offered additional care.

As we pass this point on the freeway, he gets excited. "I want to go up and over and then there and around she ... you know, and ... like that." He looks at me and sees my bafflement. He takes his hand from mine, leans close and taps me on the arm. "That place you like."

His meaning clicks in my head. "You mean church. You want to go to church."

His smile is big, beaming and he nods. "Yes, church, and sing. See my... people."

"Oh Daddy, I can't take you to church. It isn't open today and since you moved, and I moved, it is a hundred-mile drive for me to get you and then get there and get you back home and me back home."

His smile fades. His eyes sadden. Then, just for me, he brightens a mite.

"That's okay," he says and pats my hand again. "That's okay."

I push back tears and stick a tape in the player. It is full of choruses we sang at church. Dad and I belt out harmony for the next forty minutes, with him showing off his still tremendous breath control. His smile has returned when the music isn't making him cry with pleasure.

When we arrive at the ranch, park and get out of the car, four munchkins come hurtling out their door and run pell-mell to greet us. Two ram into Dad's knees, two into mine. These are four of my eight grandchildren and Dad loves to see them. He grins and hugs them. As I crouch to meet her half way, seven-year-old Lita gives me a hug.

Over her shoulder, I watch. Sometimes, Dad is too rough with the kids, hurts them with a push or prod. Right this minute, he is enjoying the welcome. He ruffles Addison's hair and picks up Carrie, the youngest, to give her a big squeeze. Rosie is hugging me, so the inevitable confrontation of wills between her and Dad is postponed. Everybody talks at once.

Addison rushes to my side, grabs my hand and pulls. "Grandma Lynn, come see what I planted in the digging place." His six-year-old face is lit with joy at being able to show off his latest project.

"Instead of in the garden," Joni, his mother, laughs as she joins us.

I leave Dad in the hands of my son and daughter-in-law with a brief wave. "Hi Granddad," I hear behind me. I'm so glad these precious people are never off-put by Dad's lacks.

After admiring Addison's newest Tonka Truck and the row of carrot seeds he's carefully arranged in the dirt there, I return to the crowd. Adam hugs me. "Hi Mom. Good day?"

"Average."

"That's what I thought." He turns to Dad. "Hey Granddad, want to go see my new road to the water tank?"

"Whatever," Dad responds.

Joni, the kids and I clamber into the bed of the pickup. Adam and Dad get in the cab and off we go. When we get up to the water tank pad, Adam talks about all the grading work, setting the tank, and the philosophy of the way the pipes have been run. All the while, Dad is nodding and saying, "That's really good. That's really good."

I smile.

Adam still talks to him as if he is the man who invented more efficient and faster tooling machines for the war effort during the Forties – who worked closely on Voyager – who was involved in the Sixties teaching civil and military computers to talk to each other (before the age of the PC) – and the man who, during my growing up years, led debates at the dining room table, teaching his children to think for themselves.

Looking out over the ranch buildings, everything seems...at peace.

We drive back to the house and visit on the porch. The kids cuddle up on my lap. Finally, four-year-old Rosie decides to test Dad. I don't catch it all, but she demands the ball in Dad's hands.

"No," Dad says reasonably.

"It's mine and I want it." Rosie insists. Her chin sets, her big brown eyes flash. Adam and Joni both open their mouths to correct her, but I stand, put my hands on her shoulder and kiss her cheek. "We have to go."

Dad abandons the ball, no longer aware of the conflict and wanders off the porch. He heads toward a nearby hill and disappears into the brush.

Adam chuckles, "He's welcome to use the bathroom in the house."

"But he won't," I say with a grin. "When he gets back, we'll go."

"You don't have to."

"I know, honey, but he's getting restless."

Joni says, "Why don't you stay. We'll go for a walk around the grounds."

"Thanks, sweetie, but no. I'm going to take him for some dinner before I drive him back."

Not much later, we are at Coco's. "What would you like, Dad? A salad? A sandwich?"

"This says..." and squinting at the menu, he rattles off the entire write up on a chef's salad. "That sounds good."

The waiter sets the salad in front of Dad and before I can take a breath, Dad picks up the catsup and pours it on the greens. "Dad," I exclaim entirely too loud. Quieting my voice, I point to the salad dressing. "This is your salad dressing. Wouldn't you rather have that on your salad?"

He continues pouring catsup, finally stops and says, "That sounds good."

He picks up the pitcher of Ranch dressing and pours it over the catsup, quickly making something that resembles thousand-island. He spears a piece of lettuce with his fork, puts it in his mouth and his face registers bliss. "That's good."

We sing on the way back to Dad's new home. Before we exit the freeway, he says, "Where are we going?"

"Back to your place."

"Are you going to leave me?"

"Yes, Frances is waiting."

"Frances?"

"Yes, your new girlfriend. She gets very upset when you go away."

"My girl. Yes. I ... need her. She's ... she..." A moment's silence ensues before he says, "Will you go in with me?"

"Of course."

The facility is plush with deep, beautiful carpets spread over teak floors and heavy drapes pulled away from the windows, so the residents can see outside. Through a double set of glass doors, I can see the patio. Dad can too. Frances is there. He doesn't even say good-bye but makes a beeline out to his "girl."

At home that night, I muse over how tired I am, how tired I am every Saturday night. There is no causal reason. I do nothing but sit on my behind either driving or holding kids. There is no physical labor involved in the day. Dad is always undemanding, wanting only to be with me or my sis or my brother. He's not as lively now that they've put him on a medicine to calm him down but still his sweet self.

Several minutes elapse before the truth drops into my head.

Friday night I begin to brace. And I continue to remain on high alert all day Saturday. The day I spend with Dad—and Alzheimer's disease.

CLIFF & CLARA

A little reminder…

By Allyn Schuyler

Clara Bicker's eyes sprang open moments before the alarm jangled. She'd rarely changed her waking hour these past seventy-odd years and didn't really need the clock at all. She reached around to pat the warm backside still nestled against her own, cleared her throat and muttered, "Wake up, Cliff. Day's awastin'." When her feet hit the floor, she could still hear the undisturbed snuffle of his familiar snore.

By the time her husband of fifty-five years shuffled into the small, warm kitchen Clara was dressed and putting the finishing touches on a full breakfast. Her long, mostly-gray hair was twisted into a knot high on her head and she wore a loose, faded shift she reserved strictly for working around the house. Bacon drained on a paper towel and strong, dark coffee perked on the stove. Cliff and Clara had done without a new-fangled coffee machine—it didn't make the coffee hot enough for their taste.

Cliff put his arm around his soft, round, aproned wife and pressed his stubbly face into her neck. "Mornin', my little yellow bird." Clara twisted out of his embrace and snapped him with her cup towel. "Sit down, Mr. Charm, and eat while it's hot. Let those eggs get cold and see if I cook again today!"

Cliff slipped into his place at the oil-clothed table while Clara served the coffee into thick café cups the two bought when they were newly-wed. He poured the steaming hot liquid into his saucer to cool and lifted it to his lips for a sip. Clara shook her head, still disliking his slurping after all these years, but completely oblivious to the smacking noise she made with every chew.

"Delicious, as always, Sweetie. How did I ever manage to snag the best cook in the county?" he teased before he took a big bite of sourdough biscuit.

After breakfast, Cliff set about some chores. He moved slowly and stiffly from too many years of hard work as the middle school janitor. His glasses made his eyes appear a little too large, but they were kind eyes and his smile was easy to return. His perennial cheery disposition had made him a favorite around the campus. He always enjoyed working around the kids and sorely missed them after he retired. Every year one or two of them somehow worked their way into his heart and became his favorites. Retirement was only hard in that he missed those young ones so.

Cliff whistled while he worked, which rankled Clara's nerves. No matter how fast Cliff worked, it was never quite fast enough for Clara. She never knew how badly Cliff's arthritis had pained him the last few years because he never complained, and Clara didn't want to imagine.

"What in the **world** could he be talking to himself about **now**," she grumbled as she watched him with worried curiosity from the window. Cliff was puttering around outside by some fruit trees, pointing now and then and muttering to himself. Clara strained to make out his words but, unable to discern his utterances, went back to her dishes with a huff.

"Now, this is what they call a choke cherry tree. No, it doesn›t mean the cherries make you choke. How about we google it when we go inside, okay?»

You see, Cliff liked to pretend he had one of the children in tow when he was outside alone. He never let on to Clara about this little game he liked to play. She might think his mind was going or he was a stone's throw away from the loony bin. He wouldn't ever worry his Clara on purpose. No, he would keep this little diversion to himself.

When he came inside around ten o'clock Clara had already cleared away the breakfast dishes, done several loads of laundry and scrubbed both bathrooms clean as a whistle, the whole while stewing over the imaginary circles she'd worked around her husband.

"I cleaned out all the bird feeders and filled them with fresh seed, Hon. Want to sit outside with our coffee and bird-watch?"

"Sounds right nice, Clifford, but I've got work to do around here. We're not retired from housework, after all."

"I'll help you, Clara, my belle. Just make me a list." But Clara didn't, as she couldn't stop long enough to make one out and couldn't understand why Cliff needed one anyway.

"Have you seen the sunflowers out back, Hon?" Cliff and Clara were back at the little kitchen table having lunch. "They sure did come up plentiful this year. I'd like to see one in your hair."

But Clara didn't much enjoy being outdoors, and the scorching summer sun was not the reason why. This wasn't the house they had started out in as a young family. That home had spacious rooms and an ample yard, perfect for raising the children Cliff and Clara had hoped to have. When it became obvious their wish was not going to come true, they had moved to something smaller and easier to maintain.

Clara pushed her chair away from the table, gathered up dishes, and clanked them down in the sink. "Oh, nonsense. They're as big as usual, no more or less. And you know yellow's not my color. It would look terrible on me. The Dress Smart lady says I'm a winter, not a summer. No, yellow isn't good on me at all."

"Winter, schminter. You're lovely in every color in my book, especially yellow," and he reached for her from his chair. Clara swatted him away and plunged her hands into the soapy water. She never let Cliff buy her a dishwasher. Taking care of the kitchen and everything in it was what she did, part of who she was, and she saw no sense in giving any of her responsibilities up to anyone or anything. Besides, it seemed like a waste to get such a contraption for just the two of them.

In the afternoon Cliff and Clara hid from the sweltering heat in their cool, dark living room on matching recliners. Cliff channel-surfed, lingering only a wink on one station before clicking up or down again.

"Puh-leese, Cliff, give me the remote! You're driving me crazy with that thing," Clara pleaded. Cliff stopped at the home shopping channel.

"You just want to tune in your boyfriend, Bob Barker," he joked. "Look at that beautiful yellow sweater they're selling today, Sweetie. I'd be tickled to buy it for you. You know you have a birthday coming up."

Clara didn't respond, only rolled her eyes, feeling neither pretty nor like a summer complexion.

That night Clara dreamt of youth and first love. She relived the first night she and Cliff met at the Saturday night dance, how handsome he'd looked in his crisp white shirt and slicked-back hair. He had been so shy when he asked her to dance that his cheeks flushed crimson with excitement. In her recollection, Clara wore a yellow sundress and felt Cliff's hand on her back just above the sash tied in a bow. She didn't want the dream to end, and in her sleep state, willed the waltz to go on and on. Clara was filled with a joy she had set aside during her waking hours for far too long. *When my time comes, I want to die dancing this dance.* This was her last thought before her eyes popped open, as always only seconds before the clock went off.

That morning Clara swished around the kitchen with a spring in her step, still thinking about dancing in her dream. She was filled with a peaceful contentment and, for once, didn't struggle against the loneliness that constantly played out in her critical nature.

She made oatmeal, fried an egg and scrambled another so she could give Cliff his choice without making him wait. She set out the coffee cups and smiled, remembering the day they brought them home and paused for a moment, amazed at how they'd lasted so long. She called once, twice and after the third time walked into the bedroom to find he hadn't even rolled over. When she went to call the ambulance, she had already kissed his cheek and held his hand and knew he would not wake up.

A little while later, when they needed Cliff's social security number, Clara went to his top dresser drawer and noticed a flat, square box. Inside she found a bright yellow scarf with sweet peas around the border. There was no card, only a folded-up piece of paper with directions showing how to wear it in several different ways.

That afternoon, through her tears, Clara tried them all.

LIKE A LAMB

By Joyce Holdread

It was Good Friday. Raquel and I stood along the edge of the dusty, potholed road in San Ildefonso, a rural hamlet in the heart of Central Mexico. The men gathered in somber groups, conversing in subdued tones, while the women kept tabs on the children weaving in and out of this expectant crowd. The women had donned their traditional best—a full, bright, calf-length skirt and short-sleeved blouse with cross-stitched bodice. White, straw cowboy hats, encircled with bright ribbons hanging over the back brims, added the final flourish.

All at once, the *Pascua* procession appeared. Village men carried life-size statues of Our Lady of Guadalupe followed by a bloody Jesus riveted to his cross. We fell in line behind the leaders to tread the *Via Dolorosa,* winding through cobbled streets to the parish chapel. We solemnly filed in to sit on rough-hewn benches set on a dark earthen floor.

The priest, a bearded, older man in full regalia, began the Good Friday mass. Villagers read with visceral acumen the account of Jesus' agony in the garden, arrest, scourging, and crucifixion. I shuddered as iron spikes were driven into the cross; the impact felt as quavering blows in the ground under my feet. Jesus' final words, "It is finished. Into your hands I commit my spirit," echoed through the musty air. Good Friday pulsed with raw, unsheathed realism.

Raquel and I exited into the warm sunshine of late afternoon in this isolated, indigenous region. This was my first-year teaching high-school students with the non-profit organization El Puente de Esperanza (The Bridge of Hope). Raquel, one of my students, had invited me to spend Holy Week with her family.

"Let's head over to my parents' barbeque restaurant. It's the weekend, so the place will be crowded. My dad's really good at barbequed lamb."

The red and white, long, squat structure was brimming with the potent smells of searing meat, pungent sauce, and strong tobacco. Townsmen crowded into the smoke-filled interior to eat, listen to their favorite *mariachi* bands, catch up on gossip, and just "hang out." Raquel's family wove from table to table, satisfying the requests of this noisy crowd. We sat at a paint-chipped, metal table and sipped warm *Coca* and *Esprite,* while the impressions of this unique place and time imprinted on my retinas and spiraled up my nose.

"After breakfast tomorrow, I'll give you a tour of the town. We aren't complete hicks; we have a new clinic and I want to show you where I went to school. We even have our own little pyramid—buried under a mound in one of the farmer's fields."

Saturday morning dawned bright, but with a slight chill penetrating the walls of this *casa humilde.* Breakfast was strong coffee and soft-fried eggs rolled in corn tortillas fresh off the *comal* (thin skillet right over the fire). The deep marigold yolks bathed my tongue in rich warmth. We soon headed out the door.

We straddled the ruts in muddy roads, crisscrossed fields along the well-worn paths, and even descended to the writhing river as we wound our way to the primary places of her home village.

"We're returning a different way," Raquel said, as we climbed the ascent from the river valley. "We'll come up behind my house."

When we reached the top, we came upon a small, fenced enclosure containing a tiny shed, where Raquel's father kept his sheep and lambs until they were slaughtered. Frisking about this corral was a fleecy little creature with curious, soft amber eyes. He scampered over to the fence with an insistent *baa… baa…,* hoping to arrest our stride. I couldn't resist such incarnate cuteness, so stopped to deliver some strokes along the top of his head and down his nappy neck, and some scratches behind those fuzzy ears. The utter innocence of his gaze held mine.

The morning light seeped through the lone, heavily curtained window of the bedroom just as the village roosters began their sunrise revelry. I was faintly aware of others passing briskly outside the door on their way to the kitchen. I got up and in my usual half-conscious stupor, fumbled getting dressed. I walked into the kitchen on my way to the back door. I was jolted awake by a sudden stab to my eyes: There was the little lamb laid out on a cement slab by the door, Raquel's father looming over it with *machete* raised, ready to cut its throat. I gasped in shock, turned around, staggered through other rooms, and out the front door.

My head was reeling from what I had just seen—the woolly little fellow from the back corral; the broad, gleaming blade; the hands pinning him down; the panicked gaze; Easter morning; a real sacrificial lamb. I stumbled along the dusty path, tears stinging my eyes. Words surfaced from somewhere deep within me: "Like a lamb led to the slaughter… he opened not his mouth." My heart was throbbing with each step. The innocence of the lamb, before so enchanting, was now haunting. "He was pierced for our transgressions… crushed for our sins." I sat for a long time on a rock outcropping and surveyed the valley below—the warming rays, the soft breeze, the stirrings of this new Easter day—roused within me a renewed sense of His incomparable gift.

LIKE A LAMB…

By Joyce Holdread

Didn't I see you
    just yesterday,
soft nibbling green
below gleam of gold
  in pasture behind house?

I passed in leisure,
   caught your glance of mellow amber;
   stroked fleece of ivory cream
    frizzed as Afro crown;
   heard your cry—
    a woodpecker's doleful chant.

Do you not surge from curled roots
   deep in brimming soil of Him?
Does He not frolic in your limbs,
   echo through your bleat,
    throb within your pulse?

Today I see innocence slammed
     beneath machete blade;
  head slung,
   eyes quiver,
    tongue slavers—
But no flail or struggle,
  still as stone,
   soundless surrender.

BE BRAVE

By April Adamson Holthaus

Kate Hansen strained to see the white line on the narrow road. The muscles in her arms and back tightened as heavy rain pelted the car. Oncoming lights blinded her to possible deer or elk on the mountain road. Fear kept her alert as memories lingered.

If Matt weren't in heaven he'd be driving. Pastor John placed Matt's flag in my hands three years ago and said, "Be brave Kate." Do I have to be brave and strong? What if I'm not wise? Can I move on to new beginnings? I can't run from loneliness forever.

Four hundred miles that day left Kate exhausted. Up ahead a green glow in the mist promised—*Rooms $70 a night.* She checked into the room she'd booked, sank into the welcome softness of cool sheets and pulled the comforter to her chin. Tonight, as usual, she would half dream, tossing as sleep came slowly, remembering Matt and wondering if he'd agree to the changes she was making.

The next morning a pleasant buffet greeted her and provided a good cup of coffee. The food renewed her lagging energy. *Whew, those last three hours on the road were rough.* The parking lot view from the breakfast area held no particular interest until she saw the edge of a lake at a corner of the building. She carried her second cup of coffee out to investigate.

A large lake shimmered in the morning light. The rain had washed the air clean and an expansive view of high mountains in the distance took her breath away. Summer waterfowl were nest building and feeding, their tails up. One in particular caught her attention, a white trumpeter swan. Kate was mesmerized as it glided across the dark surface.

I thought swans stayed in pairs, but she's swimming alone. Like I always do, focus on singleness, missing my mate.

Kate was curious and asked the desk clerk about the swan. "Our swans have been part of the scenery for years; we townies claim them as our own.

People who drive by begin watching for them to return now. So far that's the only one. For as long as I can remember they've nested and had their babies on that small island. Hate to say but last year the two adults crossed the highway and got killed. The other babies were killed by foxes. Caused the whole town to grieve."

On the way to her scheduled interview, she caught a glimpse of the swan perched on the small island looking regal, waiting, beautiful, but alone. *Why would it come back here? Instinct?*

How am I going to move forward when my thoughts are so often on what I've lost? Six years ago, Matt and I made promises to be there for each other, now he's gone and there is nothing I can do but miss him. When will this grieving end? This scene reminds me I'm swimming alone too.

Choosing a summer day to enjoy the mountain view, Kate watched from the lake side bench as the swan slowly circled the lake's perimeter feeding in the bulrushes and glided toward her with a focused piercing eye. Then it climbed onto the island and tucked its long white neck under a folded wing. She felt it was telling her something. The simplicity of caring for itself touched Kate's heart as she reflected on her own life. Could this lovely creature teach me how to "swim alone?"

A new job and new friends gave Kate a sense of belonging in the community and distracted her from daytime memories and loneliness. But the nights ... *How am I going to move forward when my thoughts are so often on the past?*

Kate drifted off to a deep but restless sleep. Her subconscious wrestled with lingering grief as she felt herself thinking she was the swan. *My outer demeanor is calm, but I cry for a mate with my penetrating hollow honking. Am I valuable alone, gliding around, waiting. What can I produce? Certainly not little ones? Am I just supposed to look regal?*

Kate's heart hurt as she laid there in the morning half-light. *Am I still dreaming or waking to what I must face as a single woman?* She pulled the covers over her head. Could God be using the swan to show her "a new normal" without Matt or children. She knew her life must move on with courage in spite of disappointments, fears and lost dreams.

Kate took shaky new steps of hope as she began her day. She thanked God for using this beautiful creature to reach her heart. She knew God's love for her would not change. He would use all the circumstances in her life to show His power and love would be enough.

Now bulrush tips were yellow, and the nearby aspen leaves flecked with gold. It had been a lovely summer of warm days and cool mountain nights. Her future would be involved in this mountain town with people she cared for, especially a certain Richard Green. If single, she'd look for ways to serve others. If a new love and family came, she'd wait with anticipation for Him to open that door. She thought, *"Yes Pastor, your challenge to be brave has helped me step into a future under God's care."*

LOVE

By Diane (Graff) Cooney

Love is a feeling you cannot disguise
It grows in your heart
And it shines in your eyes.
It springs from your touch
With a magical flow,
And ebbs all around you
Wherever you go.

The birds sing more sweetly,
All colors look brighter.
With a song in your heart,
Your steps seem much lighter.
A reason for living...
So much to be done.
No time for delaying,
There's a heart to be won.

MANDY'S SOLUTION

By Linda Farmer Harris

I used to wonder why people clasped their hands together when they prayed. I, too, am drawn to those pictures of children saying nightly prayers with their palms and fingers pressed together under their chins.

Why in that position? Why not simply hands down at their sides or laying reverently in their lap? As I listened to the bedtime prayer of my two-year-old great nephew, it sparked a memory of the people who were my childhood prayer models.

My paternal grandmother was under five feet tall and my father, six foot six and a half, towered over her, but only in height. Daddy loved her heart and soul. His reverence and honor toward her became my example for cherishing my mother.

Grandma Farmer became a widow with four children when Dad, the second oldest, was twelve years old. The youngest was a babe in arms. She never remarried.

Until I graduated from the second grade, we lived next door to her in Piggott, Arkansas. Grandma Farmer had one habit that caused me continual curiosity. Shortly after she came home from work, she'd do something toward starting supper, like starting a pot of beans or putting cornbread in the oven, then she'd go to her room and close the door. She never locked the door and she never changed clothes or called attention to going or coming from the bedroom.

During the summer after my second-grade year, Dad moved us to Lovington, New Mexico. Leaving my little grandmother in Arkansas was like leaving behind the best part of me. Thereafter, we made an annual two-week sojourn back to Piggott.

It was during the summer of my twelfth year that I finally understood about Grandma's ritual. Off and on during that year, I had heard Mom and Dad talk about Mandy's solution.

I knew Grandma Amanda Farmer was called Mandy by friends and neighbors. I just didn't know what she was trying to solve. Every time my parents mentioned Mandy's solution, they'd go for a long walk. Mom and Dad did a lot of walking during the school year. This time I was determined to ask my grandmother about her solution.

I had been visiting my best friend Karen in Piggott and catching up on a year's worth of happenings when her parents received a call about a death in the family. Her brother, thirteen years older than us, had died. I had known him all my life and the news was upsetting for me as well.

Grandma was the only one home when I got back. I told her about David, and she held me while I cried.

"Come on." She guided me toward her bedroom. "Let's go do what I do when I have a problem that needs solving."

She must have wondered at the big grin that spread over my face. I felt like a faucet turned from cold to hot. At last, and without my asking, I would learn about Mandy's solution.

She shut the door behind us and led me to her bed. She slipped off her shoes and knelt beside the bed. I removed my shoes and knelt beside her. She rested her elbows on the bed and locked her hands together under her chin.

Then she spoke to our heavenly Father as if He was sitting in the middle of the bed waiting to listen. Never had I heard such a conversational tone with our Holy God. No wonder she always came out of her room so calm and peaceful, and ready to begin her evening. She had been talking to her friend, Jesus.

I had to ask. I couldn't leave without knowing. "Why did you take off your shoes? Why do you pray with your hands "wrestling"? Is praying Mandy's solution?"

"When I pray, I take off my shoes because I enter into the presence of God. That's holy ground. My hands are always fretting me to get up and get about the business of doing the things I must do before I sleep each night. A little folding of the hands in the afternoon makes preparation for tomorrow much easier."

She stroked my hair and asked in a whisper. "Sweetheart, who told you about Mandy's solution?"

"No one. I heard Mom and Dad talk about it before they'd go on their walks. They did a lot of walking this year.

Tears, the biggest I had ever seen, rolled down her cheeks. "What else did they say?"

I shrugged. "Nothing, except things like, 'Come on, Honey. It's time for Mandy's solution.' Then they'd go for a walk. They'd leave sad and come back happier. Did they call you?"

"They didn't telephone me. They called someone who could really help them every time. Just like you and I did for Karen and her parents."

A little folding of the hands was Mandy's solution. Hands locked together in prayer against the pressures of her day kept her heart unlocked and flowing with peace, comfort, and love.

What was in Grandma's Purse?

By Betty J. Slade

The conversation switched from weddings and funerals to purses at our Sunday evening family dinner.

I flipped through a stack of 1986 wedding pictures that were sitting on the table. Not one gray hair, not one extra pound, and not even a single wrinkled face or garment. I made a comment as I viewed the family members. "We look so different from how we look today. What will we look like in another twenty years?"

We laughed, made fun, and marveled at the then and now. Our son said, "Look at that picture of Grandma Slade. She's carrying the purse she insisted we bury her with. Did anyone dare to look inside that purse before they closed the casket? I'm curious as to what she took with her in that oversized white leather purse."

Years ago, when my children were still young, I maintained that there be rules in the house. Rule number one: "Don't get in my purse." I was teaching them not to take things that didn't belong to them. The rule stuck. Even today as adults, my children will bring my purse to me if they need something.

Grandma Slade had rules too. Her rule number one: "Do not bury me without shoes." Of course, she also had rule number two, rule number three … Not only did she make my Sweet Al promise to bury her in her white strappy sandals with three-inch heels, she also had a white pantsuit and specific pieces of costume jewelry picked out for her interment. And yes, she insisted that we bury her with her white purse, the one with the leather fringe.

What's with women and their purses? My mother's purse never left her side. She hovered over it as if she were guarding Fort Knox. She left this life with Jesus in her heart but without her purse. I think she will be just fine.

Grandma Slade was determined to leave this life in style. Life for her was always about how she looked, even if it meant wearing white shoes after Labor Day.

I would imagine that most people leave this world in bare feet and maybe even a bit ill prepared. Not Grandma Slade. After she gave instructions about her shoes, she told my Sweet Al which lipstick and eye shadow she wanted to wear.

Heavens. I'm more concerned with how many pallbearers it's going to take to carry me out of the church. I guess it's all how we perceive this life and life after death. Al's mother and I were as opposite as could be. I was a country girl from Conejos County, Colorado. She was a Southern Belle from east Texas. Our only commonality: we both loved our Sweet Al.

Unlike my mother-in-law, I will leave it up to my children to decide what is appropriate for me on the day I say goodbye. I would tell them not to dress me in yellow, but they have selective hearing. If they decide to bury me in shoes, I hope they are comfortable.

Back at the dinner table as we shuffled photographs back and forth, the subject of Al's wedding suit came up. Al pointed to a photo of him walking one of our daughters down the aisle. He was wearing his prized dark blue-striped suit. He said, "I had planned to be buried in that suit, but it was in the suitcase I lost several years ago. Now I have nothing to wear."

"We will buy you a new sportscoat. Besides, I hear they only dress you down to the waist."

At this time in our lives, it seems like every day is another day that we aren't prepared for. What can we expect from this journey we're on and where we end up? For me, I plan to carry Jesus in my heart and wear comfortable shoes. Al's mother insisted she carry her leather purse and wear her sling back heels. But, maybe we aren't so different after all.

Not one of us escapes this journey. And for certain, there will be a day after. God himself only knows what the kids will do with me and my Sweet Al. Surely, they won't bury me in yellow. I don't want to go through eternity looking sallow. Besides, black is more slimming. As for my Sweet Al, he will likely be walking around heaven in a new sportscoat but without his trousers. Purse or no purse, never have I been more thankful to know that Jesus accepts us just as we are.

TESTS OF FAITH

By Sylvia McDaniel

One bright, beautiful, spring morning of my junior year in high school, my teenage world crashed around me.

When Janie pulled up in the front of the school instead of parking in the student lot, I knew something was wrong. The bell for first period would ring in the next ten minutes.

"I'm going to visit, Ben," she said to Sara and me.

"What are you doing?" I asked, frightened by her words. Her parents had forbidden her from seeing him.

Since our pre-teen years, Janie, Sara, Brenda and I—all good friends—had lived within a mile of each other. Together we attended school, church, and hung out at one another's houses, with a sleepover almost every weekend. A year older than me, Janie and I went on mission trips, church camp, and even taught Sunday school. To me, she was the most devout Christian I knew.

Then last fall, after she met Ben, her life, and ours, changed forever.

In her usual caring manner, Janie invited Ben to attend service. Not her typical type of boyfriend, Ben had an infectious laugh, twinkling brown eyes, and hair past his shoulders. Imagine John Lennon with an outgoing personality. Someone fun-loving and happy with a captivating smile who you wanted for a friend.

Over the last few months, I watched as he brought out an introverted Janie, making her laugh and seeming happier than ever. She had a calming effect on him, taming his wild streak.

At first, her parents grudgingly accepted him, but when they learned he'd been married once and was twenty years old, they tried to sever the romance, refusing to let them date.

Then one night, the church elders paid her a visit to her after-school job.

"Janie, we want to talk to you about Ben."

The three men gathered around her in the small boutique. "You're a young Christian girl and we think Ben is not the right man for you. It would be best if you didn't bring him to church any longer."

Stunned, Janie stared at the men, tears welling up in her eyes. "Isn't everyone welcome to attend service?"

"Well, yes, but Ben is too old for you and it would be better if he found some other church to attend. We're asking you not to date or bring him to service with you again."

"Excuse me, but I need to get back to work," she said and walked away. Angry tears overwhelmed her at the irony of their words. Romans 15: 7 says, "Therefore welcome one another as Christ has welcomed you, for the glory of God."

When she told us about the conversation, our group was shocked at the idea that someone was not welcomed to church. That made Janie even more determined to see Ben.

My friend began to question everything in her life, and I didn't know how to help her. The ever-obedient child of God started to rebel.

Now, two months later, we sat in her car in front of the high school, tears streaming down her face. "Please don't ask any questions."

"Janie, it's late," I cried, reaching out and touching her arm as something alerted me that this was more than mere rebellion. "You aren't supposed to see Ben."

"We're leaving." I noticed her hands shook as she gripped the steering wheel. "Don't ask me where we're going, because they're going to grill you about where we are, and I can't tell you anything."

Bewildered, I stared at my best friend, unable to comprehend why she would leave family, church, school, and everything to be with Ben. A straight-A honor student who in two months would graduate high school and planned on attending college.

"Go," she said, "or you'll be tardy."

"Don't do this," I begged, pleading with her not to run off with this man.

"I have to," she said, crying.

Slowly, Sara and I got out of the car. We each gave her a hug, not knowing what to do; a surreal feeling overwhelming me. This couldn't be happening.

"Please, don't tell anyone. Don't say anything," she cried.

Sara and I stood in shock as she drove away in her clanking red Datsun. Neither of us realized years would pass before we saw her again.

Looking back, we should have run straight to the principal and told him what was going on. I should have notified my mother to stop her. But Janie was determined, and I didn't think anyone would listen to a stupid teenager who just lost her best friend.

The day stretched on into forever —my classes a blur, my chest aching, dreading the evening. Later that night, Janie's mother called my mother and I blurted everything. The next week, Janie's grandmother telephoned, demanding I tell her where she could find her granddaughter.

The hurt in her voice wrenched my chest, and if I had known, I would have confessed her location. Anything to ease that woman's pain. Wisely, my friend told us nothing.

Months went by with no word from Janie and Ben—no way of knowing if she was dead or alive.

There were other dire consequences to that dreadful morning. Sara refused to attend church any longer. Brenda's mother seldom let her go with us, but now my friend did not want to be associated with a religion who turned people away.

Me? I was forced to attend service like nothing happened. In our home, we went to church with the family unless you were sick, and then you'd better be dying. Since only my heart was broken, I had no excuse.

Where once the four of us sat, I sat alone or with my family. The other teenagers treated me like I was a leper: the friend of Janie, who disappeared with a man not of our faith. Sadly, I began to hate my religion and how they treated Janie and Ben.

Almost a year passed before I heard from my friend; a letter came, and over the years, we've stayed in contact.

She and Ben married and had a son. For over twenty-five years, they were man and wife before he died from diabetes complications. During their marriage, they never returned to the church, but became active Buddhists involved in their community, working together to recruit and serve.

Often, I've wondered if they had been accepted, what could this young vibrant couple have accomplished? With Janie's faith and Ben's personality, they were a great team and she was teaching him our beliefs.

After Ben's death, Janie left the Buddhist community and joined the Unitarian church, where today, she is an active member.

Sara, married, divorced and does not attend church.

Brenda has been married for forty-nine years and joined her husband's church, but no longer attends.

Unexpected events in life often leave long-lasting effects. On that March morning, sitting in front of the high school, I didn't realize all our lives would be impacted by Janie's decision.

After I graduated from high school, I never stepped into my childhood church. For the next fifteen years, my faith went into hibernation. Later in life, I returned to another congregation, but no matter how hard I tried, I could not connect with the people.

Now, I refuse to place my faith in the hands of a church or people again. My relationship with my Lord and Savior is built on prayer, study, and walking with God in a personal way.

For many years, I let the events of this time keep me from the Lord. Later, I realized it wasn't His fault this church didn't like a divorced man with long hair. It wasn't His fault my friend went on her journey and left me to face the condemnation of the congregation alone.

The years that followed were a lonely, troubling time spent trying to determine who was right and who was wrong, when neither was faithful to the teachings of God.

Would I recommend that a seventeen-year-old girl run off with a twenty-year-old man? Absolutely not. But what if her parents and the church had said, "You have to wait for Janie, just like Jacob waited for Rachel."

"So, Jacob served seven years to get Rachel, but they seemed like only a few days to him because of his love for her." (Genesis 29:20 ESV)

What if the elders had said everyone was welcome to attend church, but Ben should go through some classes or special training? What if they had not put so much pressure on the two of them? Would she have been driven to run away?

Would the couple's love have withstood the test of time if they had been accepted? Who knows? Most teenage loves crash and burn after the first test of reality. Sadly, not only was Janie's faith affected, but three of us walked away from the church because of that fateful day.

As a young teenage girl, my perceptions of life were just forming, and this crisis rocked me to my core. Losing my best friend, being shunned by church members, and experiencing people's prejudices, my faith crumbled.

But God never gave up on me. Through life's ups and downs, he walked beside me. Through trials and tribulations, he never left me.

When I look back on this time in my life, I think of these events as my first test of faith. Yes, I failed. But in failing, I found a deeper faith that no one can ever take from me—not you, not a church, no one. I walk with the Lord at my side through this journey of life.

"Fear not, for I am with you; be not dismayed, for I am your God; I will strengthen you, I will help you, I will uphold you with my righteous right hand." (Isaiah 41:10 NASB)

CAN'T STOP

(an earthquake tale - January 17,
1994 - 20 minutes later)
By Lynn Moffett

Long before dawn
at the top of the hill
a black void occupies the space
where a jewel box
full of lights should be.

Red fires glow against heavy
dust-laden air.

Can't stop.

The highway sweeps down and
away
at 80 miles an hour
once smooth, now jagged
only taillights ahead assure
passable road to come.

Into a cloud of thick black smoke
yellow-orange flames lick
at hospital foundations
gorge on mobile homes
unchecked
so hot they sear the car window,
and threaten from outstretched
trees.

Can't stop.

Out the other side
broken concrete litters the way

sweep around a blind curve
brake lights
skid
cars at odd angles.

Something massive and grey
hangs down from nowhere
no, not down, but stands
a forbidding soldier
a freeway stanchion
Where is the bridge?

Where is the bridge?

A black crevice spews forth
an oversized helicopter
rising
its blades beating
its light a blinding beacon
of trouble.

Can't stop.

Dodge the rubble
veer to the right
up the steep incline
onto another bridge
Will it fall?

Make it off the bridge
road fissures worsen
debris everywhere
a car at the side
buried by a landslide

Can't stop.

Long before dawn
from the top of this hill
a black void occupies the space
where yet another jewel box
full of lights should be.

Red fires glow against heavy
dust-laden air.

God's Nighttime Rainbow

By Diane (Graff) Cooney

The lightening flashed all around us like jagged spears spewing from the black, churning clouds hanging from the heavens above us. The wild wind whipped and whistled through the trees, its piercing pitch pounding at whomever was foolish enough to be out in its swirling range. The driving rain and intermittent hail rattled rhythmically on the SUV in which I huddled. It threatened to come right through the windshield unless the storm raging outside subsided.

It was exactly one month since we'd scattered Mom's ashes on the dam below the hill where we parked. Four years before that May 30th event, we'd scattered my father's ashes in the same location. It was the rocky face of the Oahe Dam outside of Pierre, South Dakota. Dad worked on that dam for 35 of the 42 years my parents resided in this colorful community.

On May 24, 1996, Mom and her friend and neighbor, Jani Goodson, enjoyed a pleasant drive around the city. It was Friday and the two ladies shared lunch out, their usual custom. A pick-up truck exceeding the legal speed limit by at least 15 miles per hour struck the passenger side of their Delta 88 Oldsmobile. Although transported by ambulance to the local hospital, both women died upon impact.

Thank You Lord for being faithful in taking both Mom and Jani home quickly, not leaving them broken and clinging to life by a thread.

On June 30th, my husband, Judd, and I stayed in Pierre to oversee the final sale of Mom's picturesque, little house on the corner and take care of her precious belongings.

When the electrical storm erupted that evening, it became increasingly more violent. Judd called to me in the basement, "Honey, how about taking a break from all this? Let's go for a ride. I need some lightening photos."

"Why not?" I replied as we put down our boxes and headed out into the blackness of the stormy night.

We proceeded straight to the area located above the Oahe Dam site. Judd hoped to get some unique lightening photos that included the twinkling lights of the power plant below us. Judd emerged from the overloaded vehicle with his camera, 400 mm lens, tripod, extra film, rain gear, and umbrella. He stood ready for action. The storm seemed to cooperate.

Meanwhile, I crouched within the darkened confines of the passenger seat. Still in an extremely emotional state over the recent, untimely death of my dear, loving mother. I began a session of earnest and heartfelt prayer.

The heaviness which enveloped my heart stemmed from the uncertainty of knowing whether either of my parents, whose remains now rested directly below us, ever experienced a personal relationship with the Lord.

My father, Scotty Graff, was baptized as a child but refused to go to church with us because of a series of bad experiences in his younger years. He felt the church only wanted money, and he didn't have any. He was the 10th of 11 children, five of whom died before the age of two. His father had been killed beneath a falling elevator when dad was only two years old. It's not surprising that money was scarce.

Much later in life, Dad did pray regularly with the pastor who came to visit during Dad's long, arduous battle with lung cancer and emphysema.

My mother, Helen Olivia, was the one who saw to it that my brother, Scott Allen and I got regular exposure to Sunday School teachings. She attended church faithfully in her later years. She knew a great deal about the Bible and regularly quoted scripture. I just didn't know without a shadow of a doubt if she ever invited Jesus and the Holy Spirit to come and dwell within her heart. *Was Jesus real and personal to her?*

All of these thoughts swirled around in my head as I prayed, "Lord, please lift this burden from me, so that I'll know my parents are reunited there with You ... that everything is as it should be."

Sometime later, Judd was tired of the pouring rain and wind whipping so hard it removed his headgear. Pounding hail and blazing strikes of lightening, seemed to appear only where his lens was not pointed. Discouraged, he yanked open the door of the Suburban and climbed in, happy to be out of the nasty elements. He started the engine and moved the vehicle to a slightly different location. This gave us a new angle on the storm raging around us.

It was nearly midnight and from this new vantage point, we realized there was a brilliant, full moon shining over the capital city of Pierre. Here we were, directly in the middle of a violent storm, howling north of the city.

We sat together, absorbing this most unusual weather combination for probably ten minutes or so. Suddenly the storm subsided, the wind died down, and the driving rain turned to a soft drizzle. Low and behold, in the sky above us appeared an unmistakable luminescent rainbow! There were no colors to this nighttime bow in the sky … only an illuminated arch, almost like a ghostly rainbow. An unmistakable rainbow, nevertheless.

"Well, I'll be darned!" Judd quipped, as he gazed at the spectacular sight through his side window. Neither Judd nor I had ever seen a rainbow at night before, not in all our 58 years on this earth. This amazing phenomenon: what a privilege to witness it! Experiencing it together and sharing in the wonder of it all made it perfect.

I know one thing for sure: the heaviness I carried in my heart no longer existed. God graciously lifted it from me. In its place was *The peace which passeth all understanding,"* from Philippians 4:7. (KJV)

Thank You my Lord and my Savior for answering my prayer so beautifully and for this miracle You have allowed me to experience.

THE SIGNIFICANCE IN MY SUNRISE

By Paige Dené Wiersma

When I was a child, I would often dream with excitement about Jesus' return. My dreams always began by my awakening, in what I knew should be night; yet, a beautiful golden warm light filled my bedroom. As an adult, I have seen the same glow illuminate my bedroom and spill into the hallway from the sunrise in the East. Like many people who believe the Bible to be true, I see a correlation in the sun rising in the East and God's Son returning from the direction of the eastern sky.

As a lifelong Sabbath keeper who was taught at a young age to see God's order in the creation of the world, I still see the sunset as the beginning of a new day. What has been a revelation to me recently; though, is how this order is supposed to be a daily visual reminder to all of humanity of: 1) Our Heavenly Father's original creation of our Earth when He brought light into the darkness; and 2) Our Heavenly Father sending us His only begotten son, Jesus, to be our light in a sin-darkened world.

Now, when the sunset brings an end to God's gift of another day, I wait in the gestation of the night, of the new day, like a baby in the womb conceived in the darkness of sin. The sunrise brings with it a rebirth of my faith in my Heavenly Father who created all light is this world. His glory, mercy, and love are displayed in the vibrancy of the backlit pastels—evolving into the fierce, white, brilliance of the piercing shafts of sunlight that are as His all-seeing eyes. Each morning, the whole spectacle joyfully shouts a reminder of the moment when God's only begotten Son will return as a bridegroom ready to claim his bride. The sunrise reminds me to continue to grow as a child of God and ready myself as a bride to be, while remembering the great things my Heavenly Father has already done and will continue to do through His Son, Jesus, for you and me!

Genesis 1:1-5 says, *"In the beginning, God created the Heavens and Earth. The Earth was without form, and void; and darkness was on the face of the deep. And the Spirit of God was hovering over the face of the waters. Then God said, "Let there be light" and there was light. And God saw the light, that it was good; and God divided the light from the darkness. God called the light Day, and the darkness He called Night. So, the evening and the morning were the first day."* (NKJ)

SNOWY TWILIGHT

By Joy Wiersma

Steps that crunch against snow
Breath that fogs the air
Silence that sings through the trees
Beauty so rare

Time hangs in frozen space
Purple tinting the earth
This natural-world magic
Has unnamable worth

Snowy white, blends with purple
Lilac, royal, and violet
This creates a whole new dimension
Filled with uninterrupted quiet

Standing in the in-between of day and night
Where everything is built on a notion
A spellbinding peace ensues
Calming all turmoil and emotion

All things are possible
When eternity is involved
Infinite ideas in a single moment
A thousand times evolved

Just a few minutes of perpetual twilight
Yet here I am
One hundred new stories to tell
All slipping away before I can

THE BLESSINGS OF WISDOM

By April Adamson Holthaus

Thirty years ago, I fought a knockdown "why-can't-I" kind of fight with myself. I was offered an enticing opportunity for success and public acknowledgment in a world of acclaim where my desktop design skills would be highlighted. Or, I could choose to be involved in an intensive Bible course. Something didn't feel right.

I wanted to choose the perfect answer to say with certainty, "God led me in my decision." I asked a friend how she resolved decisions like this. "Find what the Book of Proverbs says. Answers you need from God are there."

Following her advice, I let the Bible fall open, closed my eyes, and my finger landed on Proverbs 8. The words jumped off the page as God spoke to my heart. *"Take my instruction instead of silver, and knowledge rather than choice gold, for wisdom is better than jewels, and all that you may desire cannot compare with her."* (ESV)

So, would my choice be acknowledgment for my talents or significant time studying Bible wisdom? Time wise I couldn't do both and the future outcomes of either had me confused. Reading further down the page in Proverbs 9, I was again confronted by wisdom words. *"Give instruction to a wise person and (s)he will be still wiser; teach a righteous person, and they will increase in learning."* (ESV)

That's when God had my attention. It was crystal clear what He had in mind for me. Would I listen or bargain with Him? Daily challenges were always going to need courage and wisdom, but was this my answer for this particular situation? The instruction was true, but did it apply to me?

I'll never know if any fame and fortune would have come my way. Instead I spent seven years in Bible Study Fellowship where I stored "wisdom."

Ten years later with the untimely death of my husband, this choice showed me the outcome God knew I would need for my soul.

I found in Proverbs 19, verses 7-11, other statements also proved true. The law., the testimony..., the precepts..., the commandments..., the fear... and the rules of the Lord are..."*More to be desired... than gold, even much fine gold; sweeter than honey... Moreover, by them is your servant warned; in keeping them there is great reward.*" (ESV)

God promised to deliver a "great reward" and He did in many circumstances; assurance of His guidance, incredible faithfulness, and constant provision. I think I won that fight.

Our Grand Lady: Colorado

By Betty J. Slade

I love our Grand Lady—Colorado. I was born and raised at her knee in a small rural town on her southern border. She gave me her name, a proud Coloradoan. I married a Texas boy and brought him home to meet her. I now live with my family, and they call this Grand Lady home.

I smile at her rare beauty. I drink the pure water that flows from her heart and fills her rivers where rainbow trout swim.

I have climbed her hills, skied her highest mountains, viewed the elk and deer and camped in her forests. I've relaxed in her deepest hot springs and played in her winter snow.

I am proud to call her mine. Friends and family flock to see this lady I love so much. She has loved me back. I have always felt safe in her presence—never had to lock a door at night—never had to fear.

But then I noticed how this beautiful lady of mine began changing and losing her moral compass. Once her natural face reflected inner beauty, sweetness, and innocence—but she began to crave more.

Her plaid shirt, blue jeans, and farm boots didn't work anymore for her. She plastered her face with paint and fluttered her long eyelashes. She flashed a defiant smile with her ruby red lips. Truth was no longer on her lips. She made herself seductive and irresistible and dressed up in her best dress to allure strangers.

She has gone the way of the big city. Covetous seekers have slipped in unaware and changed her innocence. A metropolitan capital with money and power have changed her laws not for her good but for their wants. They told her who she is. But that's not who she really is.

Even the national news has covered her story and other states envy her. They use her as a proverb. If Colorado can do it, we can too. Do they know she has paid a great price and lost many of her children? How did she get to where she is today? I blush at what she is becoming.

I cried as I wrote letters to her congressmen. I begged them to leave a better legacy for her children. I told them she deserved to keep her dignity. When will she turn from spiraling down and come back home?

How did she lose her way? She moved away from God's truth and called it relative truth. I believe it is best said in a letter from Jude. He writes, *"They feast with you without fear, serving only themselves. They are clouds without water, carried about by the winds; late autumn trees without fruit, twice dead, pulled up by the roots; raging waves of the seas, foaming up their own shame."*

I am reminded of a song that Mel Tillis wrote and Dolly Parton sang many years ago:

> "Ruby, don't take your love to town. You've painted up your lips and rolled and curled your tinted hair, Ruby are you contemplating going out somewhere? The shadows on the wall tell me the sun is going down, Oh Ruby, don't take your love to town.

> "She's leaving now cause I just heard the slamming of the door, The way I know I heard it slam one hundred times before, Oh Ruby, don't take your love to town. Oh Ruby, for God's sake, turn around. The shadows on the walls tell me the sun is going down."

Is it too late for her to turn around? I hope not. I still pray that she comes home. How does a small voice in a southern rural community compete with the loud voices who enact their ungodly laws upon us? I stand not alone, but with many others in our little town who shake their heads in disbelief. We want what we once had. We want our Grand Lady Colorado to lift up her head again with dignity and pureness of heart.

Burial of Frederick George Sibbach

excerpt from a forthcoming book on her Grandfather

by Pamela Sibbach Hayes

17 May 1904
Cedar Hill Cemetery
Ouray County, Colorado

Frederick's funeral procession slowly proceeded from the Presbyterian Church in Ouray. It would be a long five miles north to Cedar Hill Cemetery. There would be no shiny black hearse with matched plumed horses for Frederick on that cool spring day in May. An old wooden wagon, pulled by two mismatched mules, creaked and moaned traversing the rocks and ruts in the road, under the burden of his plain wooden coffin draped in black cotton. The brakes groaned as the driver slowed the wagon on the downhill slope of the road. Other wagons along with a few carriages filled with his mourners followed. Fellow miners joined the funeral train on foot as was their custom to honor one of their own.

The sight of the hundred shade trees, planted nine years prior, welcomed their arrival at the cemetery. They would provide some relished shade for the weary miners and mourners after their trek to his final resting place. A wooden picket fence encompassed the cemetery in the hope of keeping stray cattle and wildlife out. Tiny pink beauty and white snowdrop wildflowers sprung up among the fresh green of the native prairie grasses. They provided the only available flowers to adorn his grave.

Sabina, Frederick's widow, turned to glance over her shoulder to check on her children. Her youngest child, Anna, just barely a year old, tired and confused by the events of the day, clung to her six-year-old sister, Lena. Frederick their oldest son at eleven, nicknamed Fritz, watched over his six siblings. George and Paul, the ten-year-old twins, were quietly sitting still for once. Charles, at eight, tried to remain as stoic as his older brothers, which befitted their age and German heritage. Louis, the youngest son at four, made every effort to emulate the tearless faces of his older brothers without success. Sabina, gazing forward again, stifled her tears and grief, and tried to wait for a private moment to shed her watery misery. Compounding her pain, none of her family were able to make the trip over the snow-covered mountain passes to lend their support.

She remembered, as her eyes traveled across the cemetery to a tall tombstone, only three short years ago when she made this same journey to bury her brother, Charles Glaser. He joined his young wife, Carolina and their newborn daughter, in death only six years after their tragic demise from a difficult birth. The memory added to her feeling of loss and aloneness. With her brother and husband both deceased, no family remained close to come to her aid. The future appeared fearsome as she thought of her seven children to raise without the support of a husband. Sabina's ebony widow's garb rustled in the breeze as they stood around Frederick's open grave, listening to the closing remarks from Rev. Darley. The finality of Frederick's short time with his family took on a new reality. It would be a struggle for survival for this young family. What a heart-rending scene I envisioned on that long-ago Tuesday.

Nuts for Christmas

By Richard Gammill

Frank sputtered with frustration. "If one of Santa's elves shows up around here, I'll pin his pointed ears to the back of his head."

"I can't believe you'd talk that way," his wife, Susie, said. "You love Christmas."

"Are you kidding? Christmas is a lot of work for us. It's not easy getting everything done."

"You sound like the Grinch who stole Christmas."

"I wish he would steal it, at least for this year. Give me a break."

Susie shrugged her shoulders and walked away, leaving her husband to his grumbling.

Frank wasn't finished. "Do you remember Yogi Yorgesson's song, 'I Yust Go Nuts at Christmas'? That's me!"

The next morning, Frank stood outside the mall waiting for the doors to open. He joined the shoppers crowding the aisles. He moved back and forth, gift list in hand, and credit card on the ready. Three hours later he set his packages in the snow while he fished for his car keys. *Good thing I emptied the trunk before I left the house. But maybe I should have come in my pickup.* Minutes later, he was back inside the mall. He switched credit cards, unsure whether he had reached the limit on the first one.

With the back seat and trunk nearly full, he drove off to the first of the two local big box stores. *Maybe I should have gone there first; they're supposed to have the best prices.* He pictured the excitement on his children's faces on Christmas morning and was scarcely aware of the heavy traffic. *The kids will love what's in their packages. I can hardly wait!*

Frank didn't make it to the second warehouse store; there was no time left and no room in the car.

Hands on her hips, Susie watched her husband struggle through their front door with his arms filled with packages. "Here's the guy who can't stand Christmas!"

"I can't! But I can't let the kids down."

"Yeah, right."

Fortunately, the kids were already in bed, giving Frank and Susie time to hide everything.

The next morning, when Frank prowled through the tree lots, he was grateful for the ten-foot ceiling in their living room. *Our kids will have the best tree I can find.* This time he had brought the pickup; the tree filled the bed and extended beyond the tailgate. *The kids' eyes will pop when they see this.*

It took Frank and Susie all afternoon to move the furniture, set up the tree, bring the ornaments out of storage, and transform the tree into a glittering masterpiece. When the kids ran in from the school bus stop, they shrieked with delight.

That night, lying in bed, Frank said, "I'm beat! Why do I do this? And wait until the bills come in next month."

"You know why," Susie said. "It's called love."

"Yeah, but do you know what bothers me? I hope I'm giving them what they really need, not just what they want."

"I think that's actually what drives you nuts. You know there's more to raising great kids than all the stuff you can give them."

"Well, the shopping's mostly done. The tree is up. Maybe we can squeeze in some Christmas events to take them to."

The next evening Frank and Susie and their three kids piled into the car to drive around town looking at Christmas lights. When they passed Community Church, Susie said, "How about that?"

Frank looked straight ahead. "How about what?"

"Didn't you see that sign? 'Christmas musical drama, December 20. All are invited.'"

"That's not the kind of Christmas event I had in mind."

"What could be a better Christmas activity than that?"

"No, Susie. We'll take in the big celebration on the town square."

"But—"

"I mean it. The answer's no." Frank's hands clenched the steering wheel.

Stevie spoke up from the back seat. "Dad, there'll be live animals. Camels and stuff."

"If that's what you want, we'll go to the zoo."

"But some of my friends are in the program. They want me to come see them."

Frank turned his head toward the back seat. "You have friends who go to that church?"

"They're some of my best friends."

"Are they normal?" Frank immediately regretted his question.

"Dad! Come on—they're some of the most popular kids in school." Stevie fell back into his seat.

This is really driving me nuts.

A day later, Frank said to Susie, "Okay, okay—we'll go."

"Go where?"

"The kids want to go to that church program. So, let's go."

Susie's face showed her exasperation. "Now you're driving *me* crazy."

"Don't worry about it. This is for the kids. Just for Christmas."

On their way to Community Church, Stevie said, "I wish we went to church. Then we could be in a program like this." His brother and sister agreed.

At the Church, Frank squirmed in his pew as he listened to the familiar music, smelled the animals, and watched the drama. Memories, including many unpleasant ones, filled his mind. As a boy, church had meant sitting through boring sermons and obeying a bunch of rules. His parents were not ones to just drop him off at church and leave. They attended with him every Sunday, but Monday was a different story. Frank never saw the connection between his parents' Sunday morning piety and their Monday through Saturday behavior. When he turned thirteen, rather than fighting with him, his parents let him quit attending.

Frank could hardly believe his thoughts: *Maybe I've missed out on something all these years.*

On their way home, Stevie said, "There weren't any reindeer. Was that program really what Christmas is all about? "

"Maybe so, Son. Would you guys like to go back there next Sunday?"

"Really, Dad? You're not kidding us, are you?"

"Why would I be kidding?"

Susie punched him lightly. "You don't like Christmas, but you go overboard with it. You don't like church, but now you suggest we attend?"

"Yeah, I'm just full of contradictions, aren't I? I yust go nuts over a lot of things, but I try to keep an open mind. That's okay isn't it?"

"It's probably why we love you so much." Susie leaned close and put her arm around Frank's shoulders.

"Hey—I've got to keep my attention on the road."

4-F

By Kathy Zilhaver

Years ago, I knew a man named James who was in his early twenties at the beginning of World War II. He watched as all his buddies lined up at the recruiting station in town ready to sign up and fight. James was devastated beyond measure, left behind to a half-empty town full of women, children and old men. How would he ever live through the shame and embarrassment of being physically unfit for military duty; classified as 4-F.

James left that small town and headed back to Cleveland for his last semester of college. He graduated as a chemical engineer and went to work for a petroleum company in Dallas, Texas. He and a team of engineers traveled to many stateside oil refineries. Their orders were to ramp up gasoline production for the war effort.

At that time the technology of refining crude oil was antiquated, and our fighting men and women needed to be sure they never ran out of fuel. What a huge responsibility that was! The country was counting on James and his colleagues to get the job done.

When the war ended, it was clear their mission of an uninterrupted fuel supply had been successful. Everyone celebrated! Soldiers began to come home, look for peacetime jobs and start families. One of the main reasons so many of those soldiers lived to come home was because their fuel had arrived on time and in sufficient quantities. They never ran out of gasoline.

But for James, those old feelings of inadequacy never faded away. As the years passed everyone could see the sadness in his face when they heard him say he hadn't done enough for his country. He didn't fight on the battlefield alongside his friends.

Right up until his death in 2004 James still talked about what he saw was his biggest failure in life.

I always wondered why he couldn't see how the efforts of that team of engineers had saved the lives of so many soldiers.

The same can be said of many Christians today who feel they are coming up short when they look at the gifts and talents of other Christians. To God, even the simplest act of love, of helping a person in need is so important.

Paul tells us that we each have been given a unique talent to be used by the Holy Spirit. In 1 Corinthians 12:6 (NKJV) he says, "*There are diversities of gifts, but the same Spirit. There are differences of ministries, but the same Lord. And there are diversities of activities, but it is the same God who works all in all…*".

Then, in 1 Corinthians 12:22 (NKJV) we find that no spiritual gift is worth more than another. "*No, much rather, those members of the body which **seem to be weaker** are necessary*".

Finally, in Ephesians 4:11(NKJV) Paul shows how all these different spiritual gifts work together. "*And He Himself gave some to be apostles, some prophets, some evangelists, and some pastors and teachers for the equipping of the saints for the work of ministry…, all things into Him who is the head… according **to the effective working by which every part does its share…**"*.

God has given gifts and talents to each one of us, to be used alongside others for the unified work of the Holy Spirit. Christians shouldn't feel any one gift is more important than another. Unlike James who died with great sadness, we don't have to feel we let anyone down. In Romans 8:28 (NKJV) it says, "*… all things work together for good to them that love God, to them who are the called according to his purpose*".

I am thankful that the Holy Spirit never considers any of His faithful children as 4-F.

I WISH I HAD A GOAT LIKE THAT!

By Hank Slikker

On June 2, 1974, Candelaria Villanueva boarded a Philippines' inter-island ship, the Aloha, bound for Manila. About 15 kilometers into her trip, the ship caught fire and sank. After floating for 12 hours in her life jacket, a giant sea turtle suddenly came up underneath her and lifted her to the surface to keep her alive. She hung on to the turtle for two days until a Navy search and rescue team on board the *RPS Kalantia* spotted her and threw her a lifeline. As if to reassure itself of Villanueva's safety, when she grabbed onto the life ring, the turtle circled several times and disappeared. Besides the giant turtle, Villanueva said a small turtle crawled onto her back and bit her gently whenever she began to doze off (*News of the World, 28, July 1974; Knoxville [Tennessee] News-Sentinel 24 June 1974]*).

On June 21, 2005, the *Associated Press* ran a story from Ethiopia about three lions that rescued a 12-year-old girl from kidnappers. Seven men abducted the girl to force her into marriage. The men held her for a week and beat her repeatedly until the lions showed up and chased them away. The lions protected her for a half day until the police and family found her. Police Sgt. Wondimu Wenaju said, "They stood guard until police and family found her and then they just left her like a gift" (*Associated Press in Addis Ababa, 21 Jun 2005*).

On March 29, 2012, the *New York Daily News* reported a story of a momma bear that rescued a wildlife enthusiast from serious or perhaps fatal injuries. As Robert Biggs sat observing a bear playing with her two cubs, a mountain lion suddenly attacked him from behind. As he struggled to escape, the momma bear rushed to his aid and attacked the lion. After a brief but savage struggle, the lion ran off, and the bear returned to its cubs as though Biggs wasn't even there.

Had these stories not been reported in respected media, they would probably fit better in Grimm's fairy tales.

To be sure, wild and sometimes savage animals do not normally behave like caring humans, and these reports suggest a relationship between humans and wild animals that are more like my relationship with my cat. But could it be that the turtle, the lion and the bear displayed the out-workings of a long dormant divine DNA? After all, doesn't Genesis say that God created all air, sea and land creatures? If we believe that, then it's not much of a stretch to say that these animals acted like the God who made them.

You might be wondering, "what's your point?" I bring up these stories because they remind me of Easter. They have precedent in the Old Testament when God used an animal to save his people from certain death. As the book of Leviticus reports, on the most sacred of religious days, God told the priest of the people to take an innocent goat and lay on its back all the sins of the people. Then, it says, the priest had someone lead the goat into the wilderness. The priest named the innocent animal "the goat of sending away", or the scapegoat, as an innocent animal bore the sins of the guilty (see Leviticus 16).

Viewing Easter from a distance, 600 years before Christ, Isaiah the prophet spoke of the coming Savior Jesus as archetypal of the goat, as one who "bore the sins of many, since the LORD has caused the iniquity of us all to fall on Him." (Isaiah 53:6, 12) Even later, Jesus's cousin John the Baptizer would call Him, *the lamb of God who takes [carries] away the sins of the world.*" (John 1:29)

An innocent animal and Easter, the day of crucifixion and a scapegoat – only God can think up a relationship like that. To be honest, I've never thought an animal could be so valuable and so special.

Not long ago I met an old friend at a local restaurant tavern to reminisce old times. After a while, our conversation led to theological things and, specifically, God's involvement with the human race. When "rescue" came to the forefront I told him about the sin bearing goat. It wasn't but a moment that he butted in and blurted, "Man, I wish I had a goat like that!"

SAVING ABBEY'S MOM

By Kanaka Perea

"Don't do this," Brian whispered.

I shot him a look. He'd crossed the line. "What makes you think you have a say? You shouldn't even know about this and you can't possibly understand." I tugged at my shirt, self-conscious of the way it clung to my growing belly. "The appointment has been made and the procedure scheduled—of course I am doing this."

I avoided his eyes as he touched my hand. "I'm sorry, I didn't mean to upset you. I ... I just care," he said.

"But, why? Why do you care? You don't even know me."

I didn't mean to blurt it out, but it was true. Our little towns were over an hour apart, rivals in sports. We had crossed paths but never met. We still wouldn't know each other if my brother hadn't shared my secret. It wasn't fair for me to confide in my younger sibling, and I didn't blame him for needing to unburden some of that load. But why had he chosen to share it with this boy?

"I see you're scared," he replied. "You think you're alone, but you're not. I believe this is a life growing inside you ... a baby. Let me take care of you and this baby. I can be there for you."

My mind raced. I felt dizzy, sick to my stomach. None of this conversation made any sense. A few days. We had only known each other for a few days. My brother introduced us without mentioning, "By the way, he knows all about your situation." When Brian confessed that my brother had told him, I was upset but relieved. He was kind, understanding, and not judgmental. I didn't need to pretend life was fine when I was with him.

"I'm not your problem," I snapped, "and you can't blurt out something like that to someone you just met. Besides, people have these procedures all the time. It keeps life from getting complicated and allows everyone to continue with their plans without disruption. Like your plans. You just graduated from high school, and I'm sure you've made plans. And besides ... it's not a life yet."

"I understand. We haven't spent enough time together for you to realize that I only say what I mean. I will take care of you and the baby. I've lived on my family's farm my whole life and I'm not afraid of hard work. I can do this ... we can do this. Let me help you."

"I can't. I think you should leave." I set my jaw and met his gaze. This conversation was over. His blue eyes glistened with tears which almost caused me to falter in my conviction.

"This doesn't change anything—I still care about you. Let me drive you to the appointment. I want to be there for you."

I wanted to say "no" to prove I was strong, self-sufficient, and that I didn't need anyone— "Okay," I breathed softly.

He wrapped me in a gentle hug, the kind of hug that says, "I won't let anything hurt you." I relaxed into him and stayed there longer than I should have. I imagined what it might've looked like if we'd met before this. *Why did he have to come into my life now?*

On the day of the appointment, we arrived to a mob of men and women gathered outside the clinic. Some waved signs, some stood silent, and others shouted as girls passed by. I didn't understand what was going on.

Brian pulled me aside before we reached the crowd, "The people in that group believe abortion is wrong. They may try to talk to you, but you don't have to talk to them if you don't want to. They won't do anything to hurt you. Stay with me and don't be afraid."

"But why are they here? Why does it matter to them that I'm here?"

"I think they want to be sure you know the truth about the procedure you're about to have. Not just the information the clinic wants to give you. If you want to stop and talk to someone we can, but if you keep walking, I'll stay with you and we'll go straight through the doors, okay?"

I nodded and grabbed ahold of his arm. As we pushed through the crowd, I heard words like "murder," "killing," "baby," and a familiar phrase: "don't do this."

At the door a woman rushed us into the lobby, all the while apologizing for the crazy Christians outside. "I don't understand why they don't just leave us alone," she mumbled.

Brian and I sat down in the waiting room while I filled out paperwork. My hand shook as I wrote. My mind kept replaying the shouts from outside. Soon my name was called. I stood and turned to Brian with the best fake smile I could muster. "I'm glad you're here," I told him, then quickly exited, thinking, *because at the moment I don't even know who I am.*

The nurse chatted like we were old friends as she led me to a small room with a desk where another nurse waited. The second nurse rushed through a quick description of what would take place in the procedure room.

I swiped away unwelcome tears. She handed me a tissue saying, "Don't worry, sometimes this happens. We'll let you gather yourself before we take you back to the exam room."

I tried to pull myself together, but the tears kept coming. I knew I couldn't go through with it. I mumbled an apology, flung open the door and escaped the tiny room.

The urge to run down the hallway almost overcame me, but I managed to hold back as I found my way to the lobby. The tears continued as I told Brian what happened. He cried as he told me he had been praying I wouldn't go through with it.

———⟡———

"I'm your mom," I whispered to 3-month-old Abbey asleep in my arms. And I softly said it again *just* because it gave me the best feeling of butterflies.

Then, I began to pray—something I'd been doing since Brian prayed with me that day after we left the clinic, "Lord, even when I didn't really know you, you cared about me. I saw no other way out of my struggle. I believed there was only one solution. But you, oh Lord, you sent help in ways I never imagined and through a person I never expected. You never gave up on me. Thank you. Thank you for letting me be Abbey's mom."

A Very Peculiar Altar

By Theresa Lussi

Not hewn from costly stones or precious marble. It is not spread with fine, pure white linen cloths. Neither is it surrounded by alabaster statues; no crucifix raised above it to remind me of the great sacrifice paid for my pardon. No, it is only an everyday kitchen sink, now become my altar. Somehow, I think the Father doesn't mind.

A window above it affords me the opportunity to drink in the beauty of majestic mountain peaks, clear blue or sometimes cloudy skies; a variety of feathered friends stopping to rest a while in a nearby tree branch or partake of the seeds provided nearby; families of deer meander through the yard on their constant quest for sustenance.

I have never seen a cathedral, church, chapel or temple adorned like this.

I cannot say I have experienced visions of glory or beheld great hosts of angels. I have not heard the audible voice of God nor ever been called to a burning bush. But as I stand and sip a steaming cup of coffee or have my hands immersed in soapy water, it almost seems I could peer into the portals of heaven. This has become a holy place, at least for these brief moments.

Prayers rise from deep inside, often unexpected and unspoken, only expressed with wells of tears.

I sometimes struggle to understand the reason for such an outpouring which is not always generated by sadness. More often, it is the overwhelming sense of the greatness and awesomeness of a God, who has created all things; but the same Creator God hears the cries and prayers of one so small as I. Incredible!

Memories often pass across this scene, some sweet, some bitter. Regrets too. But all covered by grace—precious, amazing grace.

Faces of those who have already left this sphere, some it would seem way too soon: a young mother unable to raise the two little girls entrusted to her; a cousin, more like a brother, taken in the bloom of childhood; a daddy I was not ready to see go; and a strong, healthy husband I watched wither before my eyes as the ravages of cancer destroyed his body.

But a daughter we loved so much whose life was threatened and nearly stolen, spared. And we were spared the great heartache of losing her. Thankful! So thankful!

During these reflections I cannot overlook the great suffering and devastation that goes on all around us. Far greater, however, than all the human physical suffering is the loss of one precious soul, made in the Image of God, lost for all eternity. Such unnecessary loss, as the price has been paid for each one.

Heartbreak, unfathomable pain, yet I see hope and joy rise out of the ashes. Hope, because there is One Who lives and ever makes intercession for His people. One Who holds all things in the palm of His hand so that not even a sparrow can fall without His notice. Joy, because He loves me. Yes, the Bible does tell me so in John 3:16. This is the same One Who instructed His followers not to fear. Such assurance.

My dishwater has gone cold, yet a heart has been renewed, strengthened and set on fire before this simple altar. I have met with the King of the Universe and been transformed. A miracle has occurred.

And so, Lord, as I ponder Your goodness, Your faithfulness, Your promises, I can only cry 'Holy.' And, I long with all my heart to be holy. Yet, apart from You, *"I can do nothing. But in Christ I can do all things Who strengthens me."* Philippians 4:13 (NKJV)

THE BLACKBERRY

By Elizabeth White

(A letter to my daughter about the beauty of marriage)

Tiffany,

When I think of the blackberry, so many things come to mind regarding marriage. Blackberry picking has been a family tradition since we moved to Grass Valley, California when you were almost 6 years old. It will ever remain a White family tradition. But, it also reminds me as you get married you will be starting your own family traditions.

When I think back about blackberry picking, I will always remember the two types of blackberry pickers in our family. Spencer, who would pick and pick because he knew a pie awaited him in the near future, ate a few of the berries while picking. You would eat half of the berries along the way, savoring and enjoying them and the experience. I pray you will approach your marriage the same; that you will enjoy the small moments along the way and savor its beauty.

The blackberry is a fruit that creates a stain when it is touched. It is impossible to get the stain of blackberries off of anything. I pray that your marriage will create a lasting "mark" on everyone who observes your union from the outside.

The blackberry must be handled carefully because it bruises easily, and so must your marriage be tended carefully. There will be times that you will be blended and changed. Sometimes it is a painful process, yet sweet fruit will result if you are patient. When sugar is mixed with the berries, jam is the result. As your personality is mixed with Jimmy's, an even sweeter fruit will emerge.

There is always fruit that is ready to be picked. The best is always deep in the bushes or hiding beneath a leaf. There will be early fruit when you are enjoying each other, and the wonder of your love is developing. As your marriage grows, you will find that the best fruit is sweeter and needs to be reached for.

But blackberries always involve brambles, scratches, and poison oak. There will be times when your love will be tested, and things will be a bit scratchy. Those times will be worth the reach for the "best fruit."

And no matter how careful we are in the picking, when we arrive home to wash our berries, there are always bugs in our basket. There will be those little annoyances that you didn't notice at first, but if you don't deal with them as soon as they appear, they will spoil the delicious fruit.

Together you will learn the blackberry bush is wild and will overpower the land if it isn't kept in check. This made me think of marriage too. If you don't tend your garden with love, your garden will not flourish.

The blackberry ... often not quite ripe even though it appears so. May you keep reaching for the best in your marriage and wait upon the Lord for the sweetest taste of that season.

And finally, just as the blackberry must be connected to the vine to grow and flourish, may you be ever connected to the True Vine, Jesus.

I love you Tiffany and I'm praying that you have the sweetest and most fruitful marriage that God has planned for you. May it be ever sweet just like the blackberry.

Mom

A LETTER TO LISA

August 27, 1998

The Day After You Left

By Beth Jayne

You were my friend for two years. Even though you were a throw-away child and clearly didn't love yourself, many cared about you deeply. We met at an overnight youth activity at Glen-ville Baptist. It is sweet to recall that night, since that's when you asked Jesus to forgive you of your sins, telling him you'd live for Him forever. Your view of life and love was different for you after that. You were just fourteen.

Sometimes you were like a kid sister to me: teasing, pestering, daring, pulling pranks, joking around. When you were fun, you were very, very fun. You had such a bubbly chuckle when you were tickled about something. And you had a frown just like mine when you were cranky…somehow you reluctantly let me break through that to cheer you up.

You were my co-student in life and in Christ. When I'd give you a ride home after youth group, you'd probe with questions about the Christian life. You were so philosophical, probably because you were an avid reader and learned to think deeply at a young age. You challenged me to know what's in the Bible, so I could help you understand it better. Sometimes in Sunday School you acted like you weren't interested, but you were always listening…and watching.

What a promoter you were! I remember you calling to give me updates about how many kids you knew of who were coming to some youth activity or another. You knew because you were inviting everybody. You invited a hundred kids to an event that hadn't even been planned yet! Your enthusiasm was wonderful.

And now you are a part of something I only dream about...being in that "Great Cloud of Witnesses" of people who are in heaven, right smack in the presence of Jesus. Wow! Is your mind finally saturated with answers? I'm sure the frown is gone forever! And are you at last singing and signing the motions?

I really missed you when we moved back to Colorado from Kansas. I seem to miss you even more today, and yet oddly I feel so close to you. You were an inexperienced driver and made a fatal decision. I'm praying for your friends there who are so sad to say good bye to you in such an abrupt way.

I'm sure if you could send an audible message to us today, you'd tell us to keep reading the Bible, because every word is true. That we can pray and know that Jesus is moving Heaven and earth to answer for us. That Jesus is more beautiful and wonderful than we ever imagined, that His peace is like the sweetest breeze. His eyes overflowing with grace and compassion. His touch more powerfully tender. His smile more compelling than the most breathtaking scenes of earth. The things of earth have grown strangely dim for you in the light of His glory and grace. You would plead for us to turn, and to keep, our eyes, and our life, focused on Jesus because now you see "What no eye has seen" and, you hear "what no ear has heard". You are aware of "what no human mind has conceived"— the things God has prepared for you, His beloved.

I love you, my little friend. I'm so thankful that the Lord allowed our paths to cross, and I can't wait for you to show me around that place you now call home.

Lost and Found

Building Trust with Caring Acts have Changed People's Lives
(A Story for a Younger Audience)

By Jackie Henderson

Ten-year-old Bobby raced down the desert road on the bright red bike he painted himself. His blond hair whipped back in the wind.

His hands left the handlebars and he spread his arms like wings and screamed, "I feel freeee! I love my bike. I can jump on it and go anywhere."

I hate my sister. She always bosses me around and causes trouble.

We fought today, and I just had to get away.

Bobby hit a rock and the bike skidded sideways. It took everything he had to keep from crashing. With a sigh of relief, he pedaled even faster.

Why do I even have a mom and dad?

A tumbleweed skipped across the road in front of him. He veered to miss it.

Nobody cares about me.

I don't matter.

I might as well not exist.

As he scanned the desert side to side, his blue eyes spied something.

"Hey! Was that a jackrabbit with an arrow in it?" Bobby jumped off his bike and ran after the critter.

I have to find it. Maybe I can help it.

He raced across the sand in pursuit before he found the poor thing.

There's the rabbit! Bobby dropped to his knees.

Aw, he's dead.

Oh, man.

I'll bury you, little guy.

The boy scooped out a hollow nearby. He removed the arrow and carefully picked the rabbit up and laid it in the shallow grave. After he'd covered it over, he searched the ground around him. His gaze landed on a gold rock.

Perfect! That'll make a gravestone. He placed the rock on top of the mound and laid the arrow beside the rock.

Once he was satisfied, he headed for his bike. Sadness for the poor rabbit followed him as he kicked the sand on his way across the desert.

Something shiny caught his attention. He cocked his head.

A pink wallet? I wonder...

He took a closer look, picked it up and found a picture inside.

It's a girl about my age.

She looks familiar, but I don't know who she is.

Maybe I can find her.

With wallet in hand he got back on his bike and headed to the gas station on the outskirts of town to see his sixteen-year-old friend, Jim, who worked there.

"Jim, look what I found today in the desert."

Bobby held the wallet out to his friend.

"There's a picture of a girl who looks familiar. Do you know who this is? I want to find her and get it back to her."

"She does look familiar—but I don't know who she is. Maybe I saw her picture on the post office wall. I heard of a girl missing a while back. Take the wallet to the police station. They may know who she is and can help you find her."

"Forget that. You can't trust the cops or any grownup to help. They just don't care. I'll find her myself."

Bobby took off on his bike and headed to the post office. He looked at the pictures on the missing persons wall. One caught his attention. The caption read:

Sherry Johnson – Missing from Big Pines. Eleven years old. Red hair, Brown eyes. 4 feet tall.

She's from the next town over and she's been missing for three weeks. Her wallet was between her town and mine. Maybe she's here with somebody.

Bobby headed back to the gas station to tell his friend what he found. Upon arriving, he saw Mr. Godson, an old man from town, speaking with Jim. Bobby jumped off his bike and ran over to Jim.

He blurted out, "Jim, I found out who she is."

Mr. Godson stood there listening as Bobby told Jim all he learned at the post office.

"Young man you may have found a very important clue to help solve the mystery of where this young girl is. You are smart to have made this connection. Maybe you can let the police know where you found her wallet."

"No, I'm going to find her myself. They won't care."

"Bobby, I care," the old man said gently. "I think you could be a big help and show them where you found it. I know several of the police officers and I know they care about children. The police have tools and resources that can help you find her. I will help you too."

Jim started toward the gas station's phone. "Bobby, I'm going to call the police station and let them know what you found. I'll ask them to meet us here right away. I think it's really important."

Bobby looked at Jim, then he turned and spoke to Mr. Godson, "Do you think they'll really come? I know they'll be too busy."

"Bobby, they will come."

A few minutes later Officer Edgart, head of the police special investigation unit, arrived with another officer and a search dog.

Officer Edgart spoke to Bobby, "Young man, you found a wallet with a picture of the missing girl?"

Bobby handed the pink, plastic wallet to the officer.

Officer Edgart examined it. "Can you show us where you found this?"

Bobby studied the gentle-speaking officer.

"Yes."

Bobby, Mr. Godson, Officer Edgart, and the officer with the dog traveled down the desert road to the place where Bobby found the wallet.

Officer Edgart asked, "Bobby, how did you find the wallet out here?"

"When I rode my bike out here today, I saw a jackrabbit running with an arrow in it. I stopped and ran after it, but when I reached the rabbit, it was dead. So, I took the arrow out and buried the rabbit. On the way back to my bike I saw something sparkling in the sand. It was the wallet." Pointing in the direction where he buried the rabbit, he said, "I'll show you."

The officer with the dog began searching the area where the wallet had been found. Officer Edgart, Mr. Godson, and Bobby went to where Bobby buried the rabbit, but the arrow and rabbit were gone.

Bobby said in surprise, "What happened to the rabbit?"

Mr. Godson answered, "Maybe the hunter came and got the arrow and rabbit." Officer Edgart examined the burial spot.

"Bobby, did you see anyone else while you were here? I see a large foot print."

Bobby looked around the area. "No."

Mr. Godson spoke up, "Bobby, you are probably fortunate that you didn't. I know there is a strange character that lives out in this area somewhere. You could have been in danger."

Officer Edgart said, "Maybe he knows something about the wallet and the missing girl. Bobby, this could be another important clue to finding Sherry."

Finding no other evidence in the area, the officers, Mr. Godson, Bobby and the dog returned to the gas station.

Bobby turned to Officer Edgart and asked, "Are you finished looking for Sherry? Will you find her?"

"Bobby, your clues may lead us to her location. We'll take a helicopter up and search the area further. Anyone still in the area will be questioned."

Everyone left the garage and Bobby said goodbye to Jim.

Can I trust them? Are they really going to look for Sherry?

Bobby jumped on his bike and raced back down the desert road.

I'm going to watch for the helicopter.

He rode up and down the road but never saw the helicopter. Finally, he headed home.

Are they really going to look for her?

———— ❧ ————

Later that day, the police took a search helicopter up and discovered an old shelter with a rusted truck parked beside it. They set the helicopter down nearby to investigate.

A scruffy, dirty, middle-aged man ran out of the shelter and shouted, "Why are you here?"

"I'm Officer Edgart. We are searching for a missing person. Were you hunting today?"

"Yes. I got a rabbit."

"Have you seen anyone out here today or during the last three weeks?"

"No. I'm by myself."

"While you were hunting someone may have come. We want to take a look around for evidence of someone else that may have been here."

"You don't need to look around. No one came today but you."

"You were away hunting for a period of time. There may be evidence that someone else came that you are not aware of. It is important."

"I know everything that goes on here. Go ahead if you must. You won't find anything. I know I can't stop you. I'll be out here."

Upon entering the building, the officers discovered a young girl huddled in the corner. The dirty child with a tear-stained face was Sherry Johnson. Officer Edgart ran over and unchained her while the other officer ran outside to restrain the man.

"Sherry, I'm Officer Edgart. We were searching for you. We'll take you to your family."

When they got outside the man had disappeared.

Officer Edgart called for the special investigation unit to come immediately with the search dog.

He reported, "Sherry Johnson has been found safe but the kidnapper got away. We must find and apprehend him today."

The officers and Sherry got in the helicopter to head back to the station. Before leaving the area, they briefly scanned the desert below for the man.

The special investigation unit and search dog quickly found the kidnapper and brought him in.

When Mr. Godson learned that Sherry Johnson had been safely found, he contacted Bobby. "Bobby, Officer Edgart found Sherry Johnson safe. Now you can return her wallet. I'll pick you up and we can go to the police station."

When they got there, Officer Edgart met Bobby. "Bobby, you are a very smart young man. You gave us some important clues that helped us find Sherry Johnson safe. Thank you."

"Officer Edgart, may I see Sherry and give her wallet back to her?"

"Yes. She is still here."

Officer Edgart took Bobby in to meet Sherry.

"Sherry, this is Bobby. He found your wallet today and gave us clues that helped us find you."

Sherry jumped up and ran over to Bobby. She flung her arms around his neck and cried "Oh Bobby, I knew someone would find my wallet and look for me. Thank you for helping the police. You are my hero."

Bobby felt warm and proud.

I do matter. I helped save her life. These people did care and believe me. They kept their word.

He smiled at Mr. Godson and Officer Edgart, "Thank you for caring and helping me."

LEPRECHAUNS

By Dan Englund

My daughter, Faith, eventually got on the phone to talk to me. She'd been listening in on my conversation with her son (my grandson) Nolan. He's four years old, and I couldn't understand a word he was saying.

He had so much to tell me that I just kept saying "yes" to everything. It would have been so much easier if we lived closer and were together in person, but—he lived far away. I told him how much I missed and loved him. I couldn't wait to see him soon.

Faith asked me if I had any idea of what I had agreed to. I didn't.

I'd told Nolan that when we next saw each other in March, we'd go hunting for leprechauns. We'd shoot the leprechaun and steal his pot of gold.

My home is much different than Nolan's—there are no neighbors that I can see or hear. Coyotes howling, the occasional sounds of elk bugling, and turkeys gobbling complete my little piece of heaven. I live in a beautiful diamond of quietude interrupted only by my horses in the valley to the east and my dogs in their corral to the south.

The rocking chair rolled backward as I rose to retreat into my cabin. The rustic, wide plank floors and the timber log walls that I'd built this place with are covered with animal hides and the shoulder mounts of deer, elk, and bears. It must be overwhelming to a four-year-old boy.

He's a city boy, just as I once was. He thinks his grandpa is bigger than life, just like I once viewed my own grandpa. He wants to be like me: a hunter and maybe even a builder. He tells his friends and teachers at school that his grandpa is a mountain man.

We don't see each other in Colorado often enough. It's easier for Anne and me to go and visit Faith and her three little ones: Allison, Nolan, and Garret, who is barely a year old. The four of them last came to Pagosa in July.

Our one-night camping trip deep into the forest was his first night away from his momma. I drove the slow, three-mile, bumpy ride up the Blue Creek Trail in my pickup truck. We dropped down into a heavily wooded canyon. At the bottom is a wonderful little clearing in the middle of the dark timber.

Together, we set up our tent alongside the Blanco River and went fishing. With my help, Nolan caught his first fish. We cooked hot dogs and roasted marshmallows on a campfire that I taught him how to build.

We slept on pads, and he made it till midnight in his own sleeping bag before he climbed into mine.

My favorite memory is taped to my refrigerator. It's a picture of us sitting next to each other on a log at that campsite. He's smiling broadly at me while trying to put his arm around my neck, which he can hardly reach.

———————— ⚭ ————————

Is it real? I don't know if it's real or not. A flake of gold in a small jar of water. You can buy one at the local gift store. They're beautiful to look at and you get to take a piece of Colorado gold home with you.

Anne bought two of them for me, with a pot to put them in.

———————— ⚭ ————————

I needed a gun. I called my dear friend and life-long hunting buddy, Andy Orals. He lives with his family in St. Charles, Illinois. From his little urban backyard, he keeps the neighborhood clean of grey squirrels with an awesome pump action pellet gun.

———————— ⚭ ————————

I arrived in Illinois with gold and a plan.

The village of Long Grove is about thirty-five miles northwest of Chicago. Faith's home is in an older subdivision that is nestled in an even older Hardwood Forest.

The two-acre lots with their landscaped undergrowth, give a wonderful feeling of solitude and separation from the neighbors on either side.

Below the homes is wetland that was once a lake. It's a common area that is part of the subdivision. It's the perfect place for a leprechaun to hide out.

I shared my idea with my granddaughter, Allison, and invited her to go hunting with us.

I woke early on St Patrick's day morning. Found a shovel and the perfect spot.

The gold cache was just shallow enough. I marked the soft moist soil with a velour shamrock that Faith had made for me.

I carried the rifle. It was too big for Nolan and he was too young to carry anyway.

The three of us stealthily worked our way around the yard. We slowly and quietly snuck into the woods. The ground was wet and there was no wind. It was perfect stalking weather. We walked, silently, with anticipation.

Alert and focused, the three of us crept up on a swampy spot along the common area.

No leprechauns yet. Maybe they were already in hiding for the day?

I nodded at Allison. She began to guide her brother toward the fuzzy green shamrock.

Nolen's eyes were as big as saucers. He pointed at the shamrock, shocked. He ran over, in awe, and grabbed it off the ground. Giddy with joy, he jumped up and down. I put my hands on his shoulders to calm him down.

"Wait, wait. Look at the ground. The soil looks like it's been disturbed."

We looked closer. I helped him start digging as he didn't want to get his hands dirty.

The gold revealed itself—Colorado nuggets became rainbow booty. It glittered in the bottom of the hole.

He was ecstatic with triumph and joy. We'd found the Leprechaun's gold

"I have to tell my mom!"

We made a mad dash for the house. Racing with excitement, Nolan yelled for his mom. "We're gonna be on the news, we're gonna be on the news!"

His dad came out to see what all the noise was about. I don't think I had ever seen Jim so excited for his son.

Allison looked at me and smiled. She rolled her eyes and I winked back.

THE PROWLING LION

By Neal Johnson

The doctor looked at me lying in bed and shook his head, "We can't find what's wrong, but obviously you've had a major trauma."

Exceptionally frightening, even life-threatening incidents on active duty were rare for me. But the one related here is a marked exception. It also had deeply disturbing faith implications that caused me to draw back from sharing. I thought about talking candidly with the doctor, but quickly discarded that idea. The young doctor, obviously an unseasoned, newly-minted Navy officer, could never relate to my inner pain. Perhaps the chaplain could, but later … much later.

In the early 1970s, the downtown US military compound in Taipei, Taiwan, sat like a small island in the midst of a sea of swirling humanity. Rickshaws, bicycles, motorcycles and ox-drawn carts, primitive overloaded Lorries and cars all fought their way through the clogged, chaotic dirt roads. Horns blared, people shouted, animals bleated, all in a deafening cacophony. Coolie-hatted, pajama-clad people milled everywhere: Men pushing food carts to the market; women laden with heavy baskets hanging from either end of stout poles across their shoulders; children naked from the waist down played in the filthy *binjo* ditches; and uniformed, armed Chinese soldiers and police watched for trouble.

As the sole Navy lawyer stationed on Taiwan, my Commanding Officer (CO) ordered me to convene a General Court Martial. Ordinarily that would be pretty routine. But this trial was different, quite different. The charges here were so controversial and disturbing that we had to fly other Navy lawyers and military judges in from Subic Bay, Philippines, for the trial.

Chief Sanders was accused of pimping dependent daughters and wives of our service men to high level Chinese officials on Taiwan and to Japanese businessmen who flew to the island for sex tourism.

Sanders had the assistance of Petty Officer Tyler and two local Taiwanese women who prepared the young American girls and housewives for their trysts. To further complicate the already tragic situation, the Chinese Mafia controlled the entire enterprise.

Before trial, I had the Chief and Tyler brought from the brig to the court room. About an hour into the proceedings, Sanders complained of severe stomach pains. His lawyer insisted his client could not proceed, so the presiding Judge and my Executive Officer (the XO) ordered me to take him to the Navy Hospital on the outskirts of Taipei for evaluation.

Foolishly, I did so alone. Sanders sat right behind me in the back seat, handcuffed. To get to the Navy Hospital we had to plunge into the endless traffic with its hordes of moving humanity. As I sat on my horn and negotiated the traffic, I found it impossible to keep a watchful eye on Sanders.

Finally arriving at the hospital, I drove to the Emergency entrance and gladly delivered Sanders to the doctor on duty. After a brief examination, the doctor found nothing wrong with Sanders. He was obviously malingering to avoid the trial. The doctor then directed me to return Sanders to the court room.

I did so, but as I put him in the back seat it became painfully clear to me that Sanders now had an excellent opportunity to avoid decades in prison. He only needed to slip his cuffs like a garrote over my neck, strangle me, then escape into the huge crowds milling around us, and disappear forever into Asia through his mafia contacts.

My situation was highly dangerous. I had a large, burley, evil man behind me who had a clear motive to kill me. My pulse raced, and I broke into a cold sweat. I tried to remain calm, but I was scared to death! I tried to keep an eye on Sanders, but the chaotic traffic continually thwarted me. My anxiety bordered on outright panic. I expected to die at any moment!

I felt enormous relief when I finally pulled past the two armed sentries at the compound gate. I drove straight to the headquarters building to resume the court martial. As I shut off the engine, I took a minute to calm my trembling hands and say a prayer of thanks. I slowly got out of the car and let my shaky legs find their footing. Then I turned to let Sanders out. He was leaning against the back door and, when I opened it, he tumbled onto the asphalt— dead.

General chaos ensued. The judge immediately suspended the trial and my XO ordered me to conduct a formal investigation to find out what happened. He further instructed me to work directly with the NIS (Naval Investigative Services; today's NCIS) and the medical examiner.

Photographs were taken, then the military police carried the body to a make-shift, refrigerated morgue for autopsy. I attended the autopsy (my first), truly a gruesome experience. To my shame, my stomach violently revolted as they sliced and diced the Chief, then bagged his body parts for analysis at the Navy lab in DC.

Events moved so quickly that day! As Sanders fell onto the asphalt dead, I had stared in disbelief and shock! I had not spoken with him during the ride back because of the traffic and my own personal terror, but questions now flooded my mind: How had he died? Murdered? After all, he worked with the Chinese Mafia and had told us he would name names at the court martial—names of the mafia ring leaders and the complicit high Chinese officials.

Once alone, reality hit me. I started shaking violently and felt lightheaded and nauseated. I broke into a cold sweat again, scared and confused. Although determined to do my duty, to find the murderers and name names, questions again haunted me … might "they" want me dead, too, to keep the facts of my investigation from coming out? And might my own wife, stationed in Taipei with me, be in danger as well? Would God allow that? How valuable is my life to Him—and how vulnerable to these predatory monsters?

This wasn't what they taught us at law school or Naval Justice School. This was the stuff of fiction, not reality. Sure, I knew there was "evil" in the world, but until today I had not seen it up-close and personal. As I stared at Sander's distorted face on the asphalt and then saw him splayed open, evil and its threat to me and mine, ceased to be academic. Contrary to everything I had been taught to believe in, I suddenly realized that the Dark Side of life is a tangible reality, all-pervasive and a constant threat to me, my survival, and my family. As such, it requires—no—demands, my constant vigilance and alertness to the dangers all around.

My understanding of Scripture also took a quantum leap. From the easy American Christianity I had grown up with, the concept of Spiritual Warfare had been largely theoretical and hardly relevant to my life. I lived in a Christian cocoon and suddenly that bubble had been burst. The Reality (with a capital R) of Satan and his demons, of his insatiable desire to hurt and destroy us, and of my powerlessness to thwart him overwhelmed me. My rose-colored glasses were shattered, and I saw Satan's handiwork among the teaming throngs of humanity all around me. The Reality of the Bible's warnings pounced on me and threatened all that I held dear.

The succeeding weeks continued to be quite scary and traumatic. After being saturated with the grim investigation each day, I walked the dark streets of Taipei each night going from the compound back to our hotel. During those walks, I continually fought my fear and dread. And I prayed deeply. I knew from military intelligence that "they," the vicious mafia murderers, stalked my every move and could, at any moment, spring from the shadows onto me. Thank, God, they didn't! But I've not been the same since!

I am pleased to say that the NIS eventually broke the case with the assistance of the Chinese military and civilian authorities. We learned that Sanders's side-kick, Petty Officer Tyler, had been threatened by the mafia with torture and death if he did not put a lethal poison into Sanders's breakfast the morning of the trial.

In the end, the matter was quietly disposed of by high Chinese officials who sent the two Taiwanese ladies (without trial) to the neighboring island to be "comfort ladies" to their military troops; and by US authorities who whisked Tyler off of the island along with the American wives and daughters who had been compromised.

For the rest of us, the trauma persisted. We stayed in constant fear and anxiety for our own safety and that of our dependents from a ruthless, unseen foe. For me, from the initial car ride to my own departure from Taiwan, I was constantly looking over my shoulder. I still am.

"Be self-controlled and alert. Your enemy the devil prowls around like a roaring lion looking for someone to devour. Resist him, standing firm in faith." (1 Pet. 5:8-9; NIV)

Mommy, Do Angels Smoke?

By Hank Slikker

Five-year-old Rachel sat in the back seat with her two older sisters. Their mother and father sat in front. Their large red Suburban had no air conditioning except for the dry hot desert wind blowing through the open windows.

The family drove south from Laredo on highway 85 heading home to San Luis Potosi, in central Mexico. Since her parents worked as urban missionaries in their community, the family of five made the 900-mile round trip twice a year to check-in with the national authorities.

About two hours into their drive home, the Suburban began to sputter and suddenly quit. Rachel's father managed to pull the car onto the shoulder and got out.

She watched him as he opened the hood. He returned a few minutes later to say he believed the fuel pump had failed, so the family sat stranded in the desert with no phone service or gas stations for at least another two hours down the highway.

Rachel had always been a quiet girl – more contemplative and pensive than anything else – and sat quietly, listening as the family talked about their predicament. She did not grow up protected and often accompanied her father and sisters to the local prison visiting needy inmates or traveling to the outer country villages to attend the villagers' needs. Maybe because she had experienced similar predicaments before, she felt no anxiety about being stuck in the desert.

Unexpectedly, a van pulled over in front of them and parked. Five men got out and walked toward them as her father met them at the open hood. The men appeared like any other citizens of the region. They greeted him, looked under the hood, and began talking back and forth to each other, all of them smoking cigarettes, pointing their fingers here and there at the motor, again talking back and forth, all the while ignoring Rachel's father.

After consulting together for a few more minutes, one of the men walked back to the van and returned with wrenches and a fuel pump. He handed them to the others, who began to work, all of them constantly smoking. The men removed the faulty fuel pump and replaced it with the one they brought from the van, using cardboard litter from the road shoulder as a gasket to seal the new pump.

When they finished, the men asked Rachel's father to start the motor and let it run for a few minutes. Satisfied with their work, the men closed the hood, said something to her father, and quickly returned to their van.

As an added kindness, the men followed the Suburban for a while to make sure the repair worked. After a number of miles, the van turned off the highway and disappeared.

Rachel's parents marveled and sat numb as they reflected on the miracle God just served them. As the family talked back and forth about His intervention – sending kind mechanics with the exact replacement auto part – Rachel, watching and listening throughout the event, waited for a moment and asked her mother, "Mommy, do angels smoke?"

A Climb to the Top

By Theresa Lussi

On a warm summer day in the Sierra Nevadas of California, we began a hike in Yosemite Valley. We expected it to be a leisurely hike, but it turned out to be an adventure of a lifetime.

The beginning of the Mist Trail was quite smooth, as mountain trails often are; however, it was to lead me way out of my comfort zone. Though a lover of nature, the great outdoors and generally up to meeting a challenge, I had no idea what lay ahead. Eight miles or so didn't seem too daunting at the start but for a pair of city-dweller legs it was a bit of a push.

Accompanied by a daughter-in-law and two sons I ventured up the trail surrounded by forests of beautiful pines, cedar, fir and oak, even giant sequoias. As it turned out, this little jaunt may have taken my younger companions out of their comfort zones as well.

As the trail became gradually steeper and rockier, we began to see a difference in the trees along the way. The stillness of this sacred space was only broken by the occasional calls and chirping of some of the forest inhabitants. A scampering squirrel or a Northern Alligator lizard occasionally crossed our path. We pressed on.

As the terrain rose, trees became smaller and much sparser, crowded out by larger and larger areas of exposed rock. As we trekked on closer to the tree line, the forest gave way to vast expanses of granite, which is a common subject of photographs and paintings of the area.

Finally, after several hours of plodding, climbing, enjoying the scenery and the serenity, we reached our destination, or near-destination—the base of Half Dome.

There it stood before us. Majestic, immutable, spectacular, rising nearly 4800 feet above the floor of the valley from where we started, which seemed a near-lifetime ago.

As the four of us took a few moments to catch our breath and drink in the awesome splendor of the sight before us, we could almost hear that tower of granite calling us to come up higher, to finish the journey. Could we? Would we? As we pondered silently, the answers were clear: We came this far, we must go on, see the top, and satisfy our own longing for accomplishment. Yes, we can do it! Yes, we will!

The final approach to this massive rock required traversing a rocky field and several feet of granite stairs. At this point, we could only entrust our lives and limbs to our Creator.

A vague awareness of the skill and expertise of workmen who came before us helped allay our apprehension of the steep climb. They had laboriously drilled and placed iron bolts into the smooth granite which held two parallel, post-mounted, braided steel cables to be used as handholds. Also, small planks of wood were bolted to the face of the mountain to be used as footholds.

Generations of hikers and climbers preceded us, taking advantage of these carefully placed features that made such a climb possible. No doubt, many would follow. So, onward and upward we continued, appreciative for the encouragement of each other and our own God-given strengths and abilities.

One small slip or letting go of the cables for a moment could have spelled a fatal disaster. What were we thinking? What was I thinking, as I ascended the steep face of this giant overlooking Yosemite Valley between my oldest and youngest sons? A huge risk, yes. A bit crazy, maybe. But, so worth the effort. Couldn't think of much else now other than holding on and carefully minding each step.

Reaching the pinnacle and once again standing on flat terra firma, we were rewarded with bird's eye views of the expansive and beautiful surrounding areas, including the Valley Floor and Little Yosemite Valley.

After a somewhat arduous hike, a risky ascent, dramatic vistas, and exploration of the unknown; each member of our little troop of climbers gained fresh insight and perspective into what lies outside of the bounds of our carefully guarded comfort zones. We are capable of so much more than we realize or could even dream possible.

Will I ever in my lifetime attempt such an adventure again? Highly unlikely. But I was filled with the knowledge that so much more may be achieved by stepping into the unknown, taking a risk, facing the impossible. It is so much easier to remain in the safe, comfortable cocoon of the predictable. An invaluable life lesson was gained, regardless if I ever attempt such an endeavor again or not. And, I carry a treasured memory which I shared with a few of the special people in my life on this journey outside our comfort zones.

GLISTENING NEW YEAR'S EVE

By Beth Jayne

It was about 11:00 PM or so, and the party had ended a little early. Everyone was in the mood for a warm cozy bed on this very cold New Year's Eve night. And it was beautiful.

On our way home, we passed our normal turnoff and headed up a traveled but mostly desolate dirt road further into the backcountry.

The night was absolutely brilliant with frosted air—kissed by a bright, fat, full moon. I imagined it was probably that kind of night when the shepherds received the rowdy announcement about the birth of Jesus … sparkling and crisp with a musical appearance. The shadows were deep as we wound our way further away from the partying crowds that didn't have any idea what they were missing. Then we turned right around a bend, the snow squeaking as it was being pressed into little grooves beneath our tires.

And there they were: a herd of elk making a visit to a snow-covered meadow on this moonlit night. There were a couple hundred of them, majestic in their stance and in their awareness.

We pulled off to the side of the road, turned off the car lights, and watched them in their charming and mystical dance of winter life. Looking for food. Looking for safety. Looking for each other. The cow elk were maternally strong, with an elegance that most women this night would not match. The bulls looked like fierce princes with gentility that only true power can allow.

We watched with hearts full of wonder and gratitude for this very personal treasure we'd been given. It seemed as if this herd had been sent just to let us know that God is busy in our world, even when we think the party's over. He still has more surprises around the corner, which may include a peaceful moment of solitude in the rapture of a glistening winter night.

There is no glitter, song, or dance made by man that could have matched those shimmering moments—it was a beauty that forced the deepest gratitude of love to surge from us toward our God and toward each other.

I'm so glad the party was over early. A greater celebration awaited us in the silence.

His Words, Our Words

By Jessica Tanner

Words bring to life rambling rivers, colorful meadows, and the sound of a songbird. They convey comfort and laughs. They teach us and relay news. Some news we want and some not. But the words we hear can't live on like the words we write.

Romeo and Juliet, Around the World in Eighty Days, and *The Adventures of Huckleberry Finn* sit on the same shelves as the Bible. Their authors—William Shakespeare, Jules Verne, and Mark Twain—are mortal men just like the writers of the Bible. And their longevity of connecting with readers is because of the special message each book contains.

Each of us, like Verne, Shakespeare, and Twain, have been gifted with a message—the promise of hope, of eternal love. Our writings connect with and live on in readers because they tap into this truth.

So, when you're ready to give up on a writing project, pray over it. God's placed something amazing in it same as a sunset or a babbling brook or the unusual way the light passes through gathering storm clouds. Inside our books, essays, poems, and devotions is the insight God intended.

> *"Heaven and earth will pass away, but My words will by no means pass away."* (Matthew 24: 35 NIV)

"A man is never what he is *in spite* of his circumstances, but *because* of them."

Oswald Chambers

BIOS

Peggy Bodde is a full-time writer who specializes in creating content for English and social studies textbooks. She also works as a copywriter for various marketing firms and microblogs on social media about the messiness of faith. Married to the love of her life, she lives in beautiful Colorado where she and her husband can be found fly fishing on big rivers and tromping around the mountains. Her earnest prayer is that God would grace her words with His presence. Please visit Peggy at https://www.instagram.com/peggybodde/ or https://twitter.com/PeggyBodde.

Diane (Graff) Cooney – Born in Jamestown, North Dakota Diane spent ten years as a high school teacher and counselor. Having raised elk, cougar, and everything in between, Diane uses these experiences to write unique animal stories. She lives in southwestern Colorado and is blessed with kids, grandkids, and three great-grandchildren, all within 15 miles of each other. Contact Diane at Dianegraff56@gmail.com.

Dan England – Dan spent a large part of his life in Chicago, Illinois as the small business owner of a custom staircase shop. He later moved to Pagosa Springs, Colorado where he uses his entrepreneurial skills and building expertise as a custom homebuilder. In addition to being a proud father and grandfather, Dan is an avid hunter, outdoorsman, and writer.

Richard Gammill is a former Nazarene pastor who is enjoying his retirement years in the beautiful mountains. His pulpit ministry is mostly behind him, but he continues to minister through the written word. He contributes to A Matter of Faith in the *Pagosa Springs SUN*, has written several articles for *Engage*, a Nazarene missions magazine, and other periodicals. Since 2002, Rich has made eight extended trips to South India. These trips have given him the opportunity to speak to gatherings of pastors across the country.

Linda "Lin" Farmer Harris published teen stories in *Seventeen* magazine while in high school. She is a charter member of the American Christian Fiction Writers (ACFW); Co-Founder of Wolf Creek Writers Network (WCCWN) in Colorado; Co-Founder of ACFW-Central Texas Chapter; and former president of Southwest Christian Writers Association. From 2013-2017, Lin wrote a blog entry on the 27th of each month for *Heroes, Heroines and History*—a blog uniting those who love to write about history with those who love to read it.

Pam Hayes grew up in the suburbs of Los Angeles and always longed for open spaces and a home with animals of every variety. Pam realized her dream after relocating to a small ranch in the San Juan Mountains of Colorado near her ancestors' home. After researching her family history for over 30 years, Pam is currently writing a creative non-fiction saga of her immigrant German Grandfather.

Gregg Heid has been published in *Colorado Outdoors* and various educational publications. He contributes to A Matter of Faith in the *Pagosa Springs SUN*. Gregg served two years in Peace Corps Paraguay, and after four years in seminary, he taught theology at Holy Family High School in Denver. He spent the next twenty-eight years teaching middle and high school mathematics in Denver Public Schools, while working summers in Colorado as a Forest Service Wilderness Ranger. You can reach Gregg at goheid@yahoo.com, http://www.facebook.com/gregg and https://www.wolfcreekwriters.com/.

Jackie Henderson is a member of the Wolf Creek Christian Writers Network and is a contributor to the *Pagosa SUN*. Her focus is writing exciting stories for children.

Joyce Holdread is an advocate for victims of abuse. She has been crafting word images all her life—making them pierce, pounce, astound, bounce, connive, charm, defy, dazzle, soothe or soar, maybe even roar. She is a published poet in several literary journals as well as a writer of creative non-fiction. She writes to capture and celebrate the ordinary and wondrous moments, creatures, events, and people of our lives.

April Holthaus is a freelance writer, genealogist and networker who has written articles for widow and senior magazines, local newspapers, and non-profit fundraising for the homeless. The discovery of hundreds of family letters became her first book in 2018. She enjoys reading historical Christian novels, memoirs, and world history. You can reach April at www.WolfCreekWriters.com/april-holthaus.

C. Neal Johnson (PhD, JD) has an extensive and unique 45-year background, both internationally and domestically, as an attorney, banker, and educator, and was a negotiator on the military portion of the Panama Canal Treaty. His passion for Christ in the marketplace is seen in his *Business as Mission (BAM): A Comprehensive Guide to Theory and Practice* (InterVarsity Academic, 2009), in its sixth printing, acclaimed by evangelic and business leaders as one of the preeminent works in the field of missions. *His primary focus continues to be on finding faith-based, innovative solutions to global poverty and bringing Christ-centered transformation to communities. He speaks and teaches on this topic internationally at universities, seminaries, churches and conferences.*

Theresa Lussi is a native Coloradoan. Born in Denver, she spent forty years in southern California before returning to the Colorado Mountains. She has four kids, four grandchildren, and three great-grandchildren. Theresa's greatest desire is that her writing gives glory to her Lord and Savior, Jesus Christ, and that her readers will be blessed and encouraged.

Sylvia McDaniel, a USA Today bestselling author, has published more than fifty western historical romances, contemporary romances, and even a few sci-fi novels. Sylvia is known for her sweet, funny, family-oriented romances. Sign up for Sylvia's newsletter via her website, https://www.sylviamcdaniel.com/, and follow her on Twitter, Facebook, and Goodreads.

Lynn Moffett has painted pictures with words and created other worlds since her earliest years, at times worrying her parents with her imagination. Only after raising her children did she set forth to record any of them with pen and ink. *Blood, Flesh and Flame*, her first published work, was written with her first-born grandson cradled on her lap.

Since then, she's been a watchman – one who peers into the distance, observes, awaits – filled with a fire to sound an alarm, a cry for people to wake up and pay attention to what is happening, or is about to happen.

She has written short stories, non-fiction, poetry, newspaper articles, and seven novels about intriguing and challenging subjects.

She lives in the Colorado Rocky Mountains.

lynnmoffett@wolfcreekwriters.com;www.wolfcreekwriters.com/lynn-moffett

Blythe McHatton, a pen name.

Kanaka Perea is a freelance graphic designer and the marketing director for a small hot springs resort in the San Juan Mountains of southwest Colorado. Kanaka's design work led her to discover the joy of crafting words for marketing where she enjoys the wordier side of promotion: creating content for websites, blogs, newsletters, and other print media. In addition to her "work" writing she has written several short stories and devotions aimed at everyday situations. Her writing is heartfelt and transparent, inviting readers to join her in the delights and trials of life. As a reader, she is drawn equally to true stories as well as fiction. *Saving Abbey's Mom* is her first fiction work since joining Wolf Creek Christian Writer's Network in 2017.

Allyn Schuyler, a pen name, is a freelance writer and artist. She has a BFA degree and has spent her life coloring outside the lines on page and canvas. A recent empty nester, Allyn delights in writing essays about life for online and print publications. These days she is hard at work completing her first children's book and novel. Allyn lives the creative life with her husband in beautiful southern Colorado, where there is never a lack of inspiration. Contact Allyn at allynschuylerink@gmail.com.

Betty J. Slade is a fiction author and a newspaper columnist for the *Pagosa SUN*. She has contributed weekly for eleven years in her Artist's Lane column where she writes humorously, and sometimes seriously, about small-town living and her husband, Sweet Al. Betty spent many years as an artist-in-residence leading others to develop their artistic talents in various classes and retreats. Her art is on display on the Princess Cruise Line and in her private gallery and studio in Pagosa Springs. View Betty's other work at http://www.bettyjslade.com/ or e-mail her at betty@bettyslade.com. You can also visit Betty at https://www.facebook.com/betty.slade.395 or http://www.wolfcreekwriters.com/betty-slade.

Hank Slikker (ThM; PhD) has written academically and professionally for over forty years. He has lived as a baker, combat soldier, hod carrier, professional ski patrol, carpenter, printing-bindery machine operator, labor leader, and U.S. currency inspector. He became a United States citizen from Holland in 1960. He often contributes to a faith column in his local newspaper and is currently writing a book on word smithery.

Jessica Tanner (aka Silver Mist) writes speculative fiction and mysteries that abound with vivid characters and critters. She has not won any fancy awards or hit the semi-finals yet with the pieces she has submitted to contests but continues to pen imaginative stories for readers to enjoy. Jessica is an animal lover and owns a horse named Stardust, a few too many chickens, and several not very brilliant turkeys. She also enjoys trying new activities that don't make her scream or clutch her rosary beads too tightly. She is a member of the Realm Makers and American Christian Fiction Writers (ACFW).

Jesse Wenzel - Though a self-described terrible writer in college, Jesse sees the sky as the limit in his current writing pursuits. He has written *Under the Magic Bus: Mysticism Unveiled*, to be published in late 2019. Safely maneuvering through youthful indiscretions, Jesse became a teacher and a carpenter. Grounded by the love of his wife and two daughters, this old hippie has many stories yet to tell.

Joy Wiersma is a homeschool student, poet, writer, avid book reader, and dog lover. She began reading at age four and devours an average of two novels a week, with her library card currently showing over 500 books read. Her favorite genre is sci-fi fantasy and her favorite activity is cuddling with her dog Nova.

Paige Wiersma has believed in the Bible since the age of four and attempts to follow its teachings as an observer, participant, and student of life. As a professional educator, she writes from what she has learned, seen, and experienced—and is most often focused on sharing her learning experiences with her students.

Elizabeth White is an editor, writer, and marketing enthusiast. She writes monthly for LivingWell Medical Clinic and is featured quarterly in their newsletter. Elizabeth and her husband enjoy life as empty-nesters in California and are the parents of two "creatives."

Kathleen Zilhaver holds a BA in Technical Journalism and has written numerous newspaper and magazine articles in both Colorado and Texas. Interviews and special interest stories are her strong suits. As an avid genealogist, she has written for and co-edited a quarterly genealogy magazine. Kathleen is currently writing her family history to preserve for posterity.

Published and In-Progress Works

<u>Peggy Bodde</u>: Peggy is a contributing writer to *Reflections from 100 Fly Fishers* and is a commissioned fiction and informational text writer for various textbook publishers, grades K–12. She's had multiple articles published in *Faith Filled Family* magazine, *Kype*, and the *Mudroom*. *At the Well: A Compassionate Response to Post-Abortive Women* is under consideration with Kregel Publications.

<u>Diane Graff Cooney</u>: Diane's manuscript, "The Warrior is a Child," is about how her family navigated the leukemia diagnosis of her son and is ready for publication. *Chicken Soup for the Soul* has used her story in two different books.

<u>Richard Gammill</u>: Rich is currently writing a book about the lives of several great Christian leaders in South India and their influence upon the church in that great land. Rich has previously written three books on world mission subjects.

<u>Linda "Lin" Farmer Harris</u>: Her novel, *Mansion of Stolen Hearts,* is in the book set *Railroad Brides—Harvey Girls: Women Who Tamed the West* from Forget Me Not Romances by Winged Publications. *Treasure Among the Ruins*, Book 1 in her Voices in the Desert series, is also from Forget Me Not Romances, Winged Publications. *The Lye Water Bride* is her novella in the *California Gold Rush Romance Collection*, Barbour Publications. Lin has a passion for Christian historical fiction set in the 1890s, the Harvey Girls, the Butcher Boys, the Southwest Indian Detour Couriers, and author Grace Livingston Hill. Lin can be contacted through her website LindaFarmerHarris.com or by email Linda@LindaFarmerHarris.com

<u>Gregg Heid</u>: Gregg's *23 Journeys of Faith* is an anthology that consists of twenty-three stories of how each author's journey through life took them

deeper into a personal relationship with Jesus Christ. It will be published in late 2019.

Joyce Holdred: Joyce will soon publish a compilation of non-fiction stories of living in Mexico.

April Adamson Holthaus: April published a historical memoir, *Bayou Roots, Legacy of a Louisiana Family*, in 2018. In process is *The Diplomat's Passport*, a memoir of a Kansas farm boy who became a career diplomat to the Middle East, Asia, and South America with fluency in eight languages.

Neal Johnson: *Business as Mission (BAM): A Comprehensive Guide to Theory and Practice* was published in 2009 by InterVarsity Academic. He is currently finishing BAM in a Nutshell: All the Basics.

Sylvia McDaniel: is the author of *The Burnett Brides, Lipstick and Lead, The Cuvier Widows, Return to Cupid*, the Texas series, and several short contemporary romances.

Lynn Moffett: Lynn has published The Incursion Series: *Incursion; Conspiracy; Glimpse Into Evil; and Lawless Revealed*. Book five in this series, *Rule of Tolerance*, is coming soon. She has also published the Woodbridge Trilogy: *Blood Flesh and Flame; Dark Secret, Silent Promise*; and *An Honorable Anger*. She also co-authored a Bible Study with Andrea Downing – *HATS: To Find Your Unique Purpose*.

Allyn Schuyler: Allyn is creating a children's picture book, *Glow in the Dark* to be published in 2020 and *Ebenezer's Stone*, a novel coming out in 2021.

Betty Slade: Betty self-published *Spirit of the Red Candle* and the *Journal of Mary Magdalene*. She has also written the following books published by Winged Publications: Book 1, *Heart Bender*; Book 2, *Heart Bender's Secret*; Book 3, *Heart Bender's Pledge*; all part of the Sangre de Cristo Mountains series. *Under Heaven's Rage* is ready for publication. View Betty's other works at http://www.bettyjslade.com/ or e-mail betty@bettyslade.com.

<u>Hank Slikker</u>: His academic works include *Israel's Worst King? The Story of Ahab in the Light of Its Relationship to the Stories of Saul, David and Solomon* and *Narrative Art, Unity and Theology* in I Kings 22:1-38.

<u>Jessica Tanner</u>: Jessica is working on a young-adult fantasy novel.

<u>Jesse Wenzel</u>: Jesse wrote *Under the Magic Bus*, to be published in late 2019.

DEAR READER:

Your opinion matters! If you enjoyed *Looking at Life: A Collection of Devotions, Poems, and Short Stories,* please go to Amazon or Goodreads and tell other readers why you liked this book.

Thank you.

Wolf Creek Christian Writers Network

www.ingramcontent.com/pod-product-compliance
Lightning Source LLC
Chambersburg PA
CBHW071247130626
46556CB00003B/1203